Ad
zin
the
col
by
the REACT Top Young Adult Read
Award. *Man Bites Dog* is his first
novel.

20ρ

WITHDRAWN

GREENWICH LIBRARIES

3 8028 01659338 3

MAN BITES DOG

ADAM FORD

ALLEN&UNWIN

First published in 2003

Copyright © Text and cartoons, Adam Ford 2003
Copyright © Map, Mandy Ord 2003
Copyright © Cover design, Hofstede Design 2003

All rights reserved. No part of this book may be reproduced
or transmitted in any form or by any means, electronic or
mechanical, including photocopying, recording or by any
information storage and retrieval system, without prior
permission in writing from the publisher. The *Australian
Copyright Act 1968* (the Act) allows a maximum of one
chapter or ten per cent of this book, whichever is the greater,
to be photocopied by any educational institution for its
educational purposes provided that the educational institution
(or body that administers it) has given a remuneration notice
to Copyright Agency Limited (CAL) under the Act.

Allen & Unwin
83 Alexander St
Crows Nest NSW 2065
Australia
Phone: (61 2) 8425 0100
Fax: (61 2) 9906 2218
Email: info@allenandunwin.com
Web: www.allenandunwin.com

National Library of Australia
Cataloguing-in-Publication entry:
Ford, Adam, 1972– .
Man bites dog.
ISBN 1 86508 686 X.
I. Letter carriers - Fiction. 2. Pets - Death - Fiction.
3. Malicious accusation - Fiction. I. Title.
A823.3

Cover and text design by Hofstede Design
Set in 9 pt Frutiger Light by Midland Typesetters
Printed in Australia by McPherson's Printing Group

10 9 8 7 6 5 4 3 2 1

Lyrics from 'O Superman' (p. 7) by Laurie Anderson,
reproduced with kind permission of the artist.

Extract from the *Style Manual for Authors, Editors and
Printers*, 5th ed. 1994, AusInfo, copyright Commonwealth of
Australia, reproduced with permission.

Early version of parts of this novel originally appeared in
Imaginary Friends, published by Andrew Morgan, 2001.

Dedicated to Anna Hedigan.

Thanks to Nick Earls, Simmone Howell, Tim Richards, Laurie Anderson and the Australian Government Printing Service.

Love to my family.

This book was completed with the invaluable assistance of a residency at Varuna Writers' Centre granted by the Eleanor Dark Foundation—thanks to all who made it possible.

L B OF GREENWICH
LIBRARIES

EA

016593383	
Cypher	08.10.04
F	£7.00

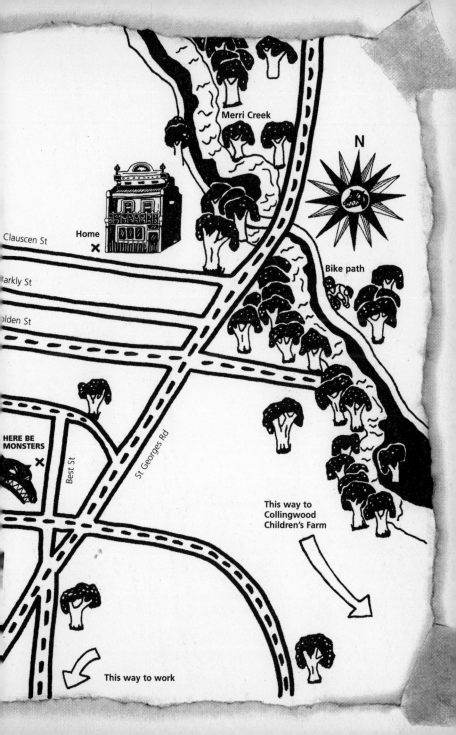

DOG

Satan stands up on his hind legs and leans against the fence, drool falling from his lips. He bares his fangs and growls a deep, bear-like growl. His paws rest on the top of the fence. His head is level with mine. As I approach the gate, the beat of his growl gets faster. I reach into my pocket and pull out a fresh piece of uncooked chicken. The slimy skin feels cold through the Gladwrap. Satan licks his lips and continues his one-note song. I unwrap the chicken and lob it over the fence, and it hits the wooden veranda with a dull thump. Satan drops onto all fours and trots over to the chicken, and in the brief moment he takes to wolf it down I slip the mail into the slot beside the gate and jump back to my waiting bike. I step on the pedals and push off. I'm not even at the next house when Satan's evil baritone fills my ears.

I don't speak dog, I've never met anyone who speaks dog, but there's no doubt in my mind what Satan is saying.

'Don't think you can buy me off with chicken, little man. On the day I get through to the other side of this fence, I'm having mailman for breakfast.'

the godlings

Hi. I'm Kid Shiva, and this is Li'l Hanuman. She's a monkey-goddess.

more monkeys equals more fun!

there's another of us you've yet to meet, but she doesn't seem to be around just now...

a barrel filled with monkeys is a barrel filled with fun!

will you STOP that?

monkey.

guys? the third panel is supposed to be for the punchline.

(si.)

MAN

I never hated university. Never liked it either. Just went there. Didn't have any better ideas about what I could be doing with my time. Actually, that's a lie. I had a lot of ideas. Most of them involved not getting out of bed until about 8.30 the following Thursday, going down to the pub to see what bands were playing, and scamming free drinks off Gina. But given the effort that everyone (myself included) had made to get me to university, I needed a better reason for dropping out than a nagging feeling of ambivalence about the whole tertiary education system. And given that I was only ambivalent—not angry, not resentful, not disappointed, not even contemptuous—it seemed like the best thing to do was just hang in there and slog on through until the end.

So, when the final day of university came around, after three moderately dull years of exploring the inner suburbs of Melbourne and trying to stay awake during Psychology of Adolescence, I found myself standing at the edge of the campus, staring down at my shoes.

I love my shoes. The Chuck Taylor Converse All-Star is a classic. Unpretentious in form, functional in function. You put them on your feet and they stop rocks and glass jabbing into you. Plus they're green. Green shoes are cool. But the reason I was staring down at my excellent bottle-green feet-protecting Chucks wasn't the deep admiration I had for them. It was because it had just occurred to me that once I stepped off campus I would be crossing an Imaginary Line separating the Real World from the World of University. Not that I was unfamiliar with the Real World. I had travelled through it almost daily as I cycled from my house to uni. I'd walked around in the Real World on weekends, checking it all out, smelling its smells, tripping over its small animals, bumping my head on its door-ways. I was as well travelled in the Real World as anyone else. But this time there would be no turning back. Once I stepped over the Imaginary Line I'd become a permanent resident of the Real World instead of a tourist who could nick off home if things got too freaky.

Once I stepped off-campus I'd be faced with the Big Question. The question I'd avoided these last few weeks as I concentrated on finishing my end-of-semester essays. The question I feared being asked. The question that there was no way to avoid.

The Question: What are you going to do with the rest of your life?
The Answer: I have no fucking idea.

I never really planned my life. I sort of had it planned for me, but not in any grandiose, manipulative way. A better way to look at it is that I never spent any time actually working out what I was going to do from day to day. It was all kind of laid out for me. Primary school to secondary school, secondary school to university, university to . . . some kind of job related to my 'field of expertise'. But after three years of wiping drool from my lecture notes, the only thing I could state with confidence was that I would rather strip my skin off with a razor blade and dive into a swimming pool filled with lemon juice than hand in another essay or sit through another three-hour exam again. I may have had no idea what I wanted to do with my life, but I was deadly certain about what I didn't want to do.

I stood with my toes resting just behind the line where the brick-paved university walkway met the bitumen footpath along Swanston Street. I stood there, caught in what I flattered myself was an existential crisis. I didn't know the exact definition of the word, so I couldn't be entirely sure that an existential crisis was what I was having. But I liked the sound of it. It made me feel kind of romantic, which was better than confused, which was how—if I was honest with myself—I really felt.

I continued to stare down at my Chucks. To the outside world I would have looked like someone simply staring at his shoes, which was perfectly understandable. The outside world could not be expected to appreciate the importance of my thought processes at that moment. The outside world could even be forgiven for bumping straight into me as it made its way to a geology lecture in the building across the road, sending me sprawling onto my hands and knees, a good fifteen centimetres on the wrong side of the border of University Life and the Real World.

What was not understandable, what was pretty much unforgivable, was the subsequent lack of acknowledgement from the outside world as it sprinted across the street to catch the flashing red man.

Wincing, I picked myself up and inspected my knee for damage. It wasn't too bad—a little bit of shredded skin and a little bit of blood. An auspicious debut, I thought to myself. Welcome to the Real World.

'Are you okay?'

Someone I had never seen before was standing over me.

'Oh. Yeah, I'm fine. Thanks.' I stood up. My knee was tender, but it seemed capable of bearing my weight.

'You should probably disinfect that,' said the person, who turned out to be a dark-haired woman wearing a red-and-silver Stereolab T-shirt.

'I was just heading home anyway,' I mumbled.

'Okay. Well, see you.' She smiled and walked off down Tin Alley, towards the university union building.

'Watch out you don't trip on the Imaginary Line,' I said.

She turned around. 'Huh?'

I hadn't meant her to hear me. I shrugged and shook my head. 'Nothing. Thanks for your help.'

The pedestrian lights started bipping. I crossed over and headed for the bus stop.

Walking along Elgin Street I replayed the brief encounter in my mind. Should I have asked her out? I could at least have said something about her T-shirt. She was pretty cute. The whole thing happened so fast, I didn't have time to react. Maybe I should run back and offer to buy her a coffee or something. No. She'd probably think I was some kind of desperate creep. She probably already thought I was an uncoordinated dork, anyway. Or, much more likely, she wasn't thinking about me at all, and was getting on with her life. Which was exactly what I should have been doing.

I waited at the bus stop on Rathdowne Street and watched the traffic flow past, thinking of the answers I used to give when people asked what I wanted to be when I grew up. A vet. A cartoonist. A superhero. All good answers. But how do you know when you've actually grown up? I was a good five or ten years older now than when I first formulated those answers, but did that qualify me as a grown-up? I peered at the cars rushing past. Were the people in those cars grown-ups? Was that how they thought of themselves?

The bus pulled up and the doors hissed open. I sat down next to an abandoned copy of the local newspaper and absent-mindedly leafed through to the personals. My eyes flicked over the blurry photos of 'lovely ladies' on offer, and then to the situations vacant column opposite. What the hell, I thought, and turned my attention from the enticements on offer at AsianHeat-dot-com to the two or three columns of job advertisements.

Chef, hairdresser's apprentice, personal assistant, pizza delivery worker (must have own car), plumber, plumber, postal delivery officer, sandwich hand, sandwich hand . . .

Postal delivery officer? It wasn't the stupidest idea I'd ever heard. In fact, it sounded kind of appealing. Riding your bike around, delivering mail, singing the line from Laurie Anderson's 'O Superman' to yourself: 'Neither snow nor rain . . . nor gloom of night . . . shall stay this courier . . . from the swift com-ple-shunnn . . . of their appointed round . . .' And then the high keyboard part kicks in and is soon joined by the middle register, following it an octave below. What a great song.

I got off at my stop with the paper tucked under my arm, singing under my breath. 'Well, you don't know me . . . But I know you . . . and I've got a message . . . to give to you . . . here come the planes . . .'

Van was sitting in the lounge room.

'They're American planes,' I told her.

'What?'

'Made in America. Smoking or non-smoking?'

'Non. How was the last day of uni?'

'Oh, you know. Okay, I guess. I got the essay in with about half an hour to go.'

'So what now?'

I reached into my bag and pulled out the newspaper, open at the situations vacant page, and read the ad again.

POSTAL DELIVERY OFFICERS wanted for the northern inner suburbs. Call 9101 3333 for application form.

It was simple, yet evocative. It said little but it promised much. It was almost like one of those seventeen-syllable haiku poems they make you write in primary school.

I smiled and passed the paper to Van. 'I'm going to be a mailman,' I said.

They sent me an application form in the mail and I filled it in on the same day as my application for the dole. Either way, I'd be getting paid by the government. The fuckers at the dole office said it would take four weeks to set up my NewStart allowance. The Post Office called me the next day to come in for an interview.

Two weeks later I was cycling along behind postal worker Jane Joad, watching her fulfil her role in the information distribution service that all Australians depend on.

'The shittiest thing is having to double back,' she said as she slotted a batch of envelopes into a dark green mailbox. 'The trick is to make sure you've got all the mail packed right before you load up. If you do it right, you keep moving forward and you get home sooner.'

The air was cool and quiet at that time of the day. A hush of anticipation sat over the city, disturbed only by the buzz of our tyres and the squeaking of our brakes.

I stifled a yawn.

'How long did it take you to get used to the early starts?'

'Not long,' she said, shaking her head and laughing. 'You learn pretty quick that late nights aren't what you want.'

I stopped my bike to scratch a sleepy cat under the chin.

'But the mornings are really worth it,' she added.

'So how come you're leaving?'

'I'm not, I'm upgrading. I've had my name down for a van gig for ages now, and a whole bunch of them just came up.'

Jane and twenty others from the Fitzroy Mail Delivery Centre had successfully applied for transfers to the new delivery runs out in the western suburbs. She'd be driving her new red van out to Caroline Springs every morning, spreading the Australia Post gospel out on the western frontiers. When the transfers came through, the Delivery Centre had suddenly found itself in the unusual position of having too many bicycle runs and not enough posties.

'Normally you can only get in here when one of the old buggers retires or dies,' said Jane. 'You're pretty lucky, Steven.'

Frazzled by the early starts, I didn't get to know the other people who'd started at the same time as me. We'd had an official orientation and welcome thing on the first day, but after that we'd been paired off with the people we were replacing. One guy stuck out from the crowd, though. There was something about him that even sleep deprivation couldn't suppress. I'd noticed him wandering in late, singing songs at the top of his voice and being all matey with the old posties.

When the time came for us to start working our new runs solo, I found myself placed next to him in the sorting area, our racks side by side.

'So how's it all going? Have you found the career path you always strived for?' he asked.

I was getting used to the mornings, but I still wasn't anywhere near this guy's energy levels. I blinked at him in lieu of anything more coherent.

'Is this your dream job, I mean? Are you gonna be a postie for the rest of your life?'

'I dunno. Hadn't thought about it. It's okay.'

'What do you like about it?' he raised one eyebrow in anticipation.

'The quiet. It gives me time to think.'

'A thinker, huh? What do you think about?'

'Just stuff, you know. I think about the people we deliver to. I wonder about the proportions, I mean, do we bring more bad news to the door than good news?'

'Bad. Look at how many bills we deliver.'

'Good point.'

'Wayne,' he said, offering me his hand. 'Wayne Jackson.'

'Steve. Steve Lydon.'

'Lydon, hey?' he asked.

'No relation,' I said. 'And yes, I like the Sex Pistols, yes, I saw *The Filth and the Fury* and yes, I liked some of what Public Image Limited did, but the later stuff is pretty crap.'

'Fair enough,' grinned Wayne, turning back to his rack.

'So what about you?' I asked after a minute or two of feeling embarrassed by my little outburst. 'This your ideal job?'

'Mate, a job's a job. But yeah, I've always wanted to work in the post office. Me and the Buke.'

'Who?'

'Buke. Bukowski? Charles Bukowski?'

'Friend of yours?'

'He's a writer. A poet. He worked for the post office in America in the fifties, delivering mail and fucking all the bored housewives. He was an alcoholic.'

'So which are you? A poet? Or an alcoholic?'

'Depends on when you're talking to me.'

'And have you managed to fuck many housewives since starting here?'

'Not yet, but times have changed. No, the sex, for me, comes from the poetry.'

'From the poetry,' I repeated.

'Yeah,' he nodded.

'You get sex from *poetry*?'

'Yes, sir.'

'Bullshit.'

'Well, check it out.' He grabbed a small card-covered booklet from his bag and flipped it onto my desk.

'*Hard Times* by Wayne M. Jackson,' I read out loud.

'That's me.'

'I've seen this before somewhere.'

'It's in a few bookstores. Brunswick Street Books, Missing Link, Polyester . . . You might have seen it around, yeah?'

'I guess I must've.' Wayne's list of stockists had jogged my memory. The last time I went into Polyester to check out the new zines, I'd seen *Hard Times*, with its grainy black-and-white photo of a man sleeping in a doorway. As usual, I'd reorganised the stock to make Gina's zine, *Zines, She Wrote*, more prominent, placing it on the top of the pile. Fuck 'em, I'd thought. The harder I make it to find homemade poetry books, the happier the world will be.

I bit my tongue, flipped to a random page and read a little bit. The poem was called 'Shit Happens'.

three a.m. in the Punters Club
and I'm down to my last gold coin again
and I don't recognise anyone here

who I could go halves with for a beer

so I wander out into the street

and the fresh air punches me in the throat

and I watch the hot dog man pack up

leaving spilled puddles of mustard

and barbecue sauce behind him

and I start off in the direction of home

and I pass that old Greek guy sitting outside

the back door of the bagel bakery

and the two of us go dumpster diving

for day-old bagels

and we share my last cigarette

stuffing our faces with dry bagels

and I give him my last gold coin

and say goodnight to him

and tell him to take care because

shit happens,

and he looks at me and says,

I know.

I looked up. 'This gets you sex?'

'Sometimes.'

I'd never thought to try to get sex with poetry. Making the girl laugh, yes. Getting the girl drunk, sure. Getting myself drunk, absolutely. But it had never occurred to me to use poetry. I probably don't know enough about poetry. I'm okay with limericks. I could do that one about the old man with the beard off by heart. But the vision of my rendition of 'There was a young man from Nantucket' inspiring wanton women to throw their undies at me was hard to sustain.

'It doesn't rhyme,' I said.

'It doesn't have to rhyme.' Wayne snatched his book back from me. 'Fucking philistine.'

'No, it's good. I liked it. It was . . . interesting. Like something that could really have happened. Very, um, evocative.' I backpedalled, wanting to be polite, looking for the right kind of compliment. He might have an ego on him, but there was something charming about Wayne. I'd never had a workmate before—I'd never had real work before—and Wayne seemed interesting enough to fill the job description.

'You should come hear me read sometime.'

My vague compliments seemed to have placated him. 'I've got a feature this Thursday, at the Jamieson. You should come.'

'A feature what?'

'Just come to the Jamieson on Thursday, about eight, smart arse. I'll be reading my poems on stage. Some of 'em come across better when they're performed.'

'Does it cost money?'

'Nah, I'll put you on the door. But the first beer's on you.'

'Sounds fair,' I said, hefting the bags under my arms.

'Eight.'

'Okay, but if it sucks you owe me a beer.'

I arrived at the Jamieson expecting something out of an old film about beatniks: all skivvies and bongos, berets and goatees, but the pub was filled with ordinary-looking people sitting around drinking beers. There were more second-hand suit-jackets than you'd find in a normal pub crowd, and plenty of black, but nobody looked like the kind of person you'd walk past on the street and then whisper to your friend, 'Hey, check out the *poet.*'

I gave my name to the woman on the door and spotted Wayne sitting by himself at a small table, a stack of loose pages in front of him. I grabbed two beers from the bar and joined him, passing him a cold pot glass before settling down to watch the evening's proceedings. Wayne got up on stage after two people had read fairly disastrous poems about Hills Hoists and the nature of mortality. I sipped my beer and tried to work out the minimum time required before I could leave without seeming rude.

Wayne stood on the small raised platform in front of the microphone stand and recited a dozen poems, most of them dealing with going out and getting drunk, but a few about life as a postie. The poems were good. I was relieved. I liked Wayne, and if his poems had turned out to be shit it would have been awkward to avoid telling him. I could identify with his subject matter, and I liked his straightforward language. It wasn't the way I'd expected poetry to be—all big words and meaning-of-life crap. One poem even made me laugh. It was less like he was reciting poetry and more like he was at a party with his mates, sharing a bunch of stories from last week. After he'd finished we proceeded to get righteously drunk, and, with me following Wayne's lead, we spent the evening critiquing and heckling the performers on the open stage, trying to outdo each other. I suspect we seemed much less clever to the rest of the pub than we did to ourselves.

The reading at the Jamieson was my first fully-fledged poetry reading, but not my last. It wasn't the poetry that kept me coming back, though some of it was entertaining enough. It was the pure pleasure of getting stinking drunk with such a funny and outspoken guy. I admired Wayne's self-assuredness, both on-stage and off. I'd never met anyone so certain that his opinion was worth listening to—even when it wasn't, which was a good percentage of the time. Wayne might rub some people up the wrong way, but I enjoyed swapping bullshit with him. And when I couldn't keep up with him any more, I just sat back and watched him go solo.

'You should get up there, mate,' said Wayne one night, after a particularly gorgeous gothic girl had finished her treatise on 'soul-death'.

I rolled my eyes and slugged a mouthful of beer. 'Fuck off.'

'No, seriously. How hard could it be?'

'Yeah, I guess if you can do it.'

'Fuck you. You're too chickenshit.'

Resisting the dare wasn't hard. I had no interest in entering the world of performance poetry. I didn't understand why people would get up in front of a bunch of strangers and read their own writing, but if that was what they wanted to do, who was I to stop them? In the meantime, however, I would continue to use the pubs we graced with our presence for their primary function: the serving and consumption of beer.

The other thing that kept me coming back was the high proportion of cute poets with decidedly gothic tendencies. I've always been a sucker for a goth chick, and I probably always will be. It's frustrating, though, because there's absolutely nothing gothic about me, and if there's one thing I've learned over the years of attempting to flirt with goth chicks it's that they treat the non-gothic with a liberal mix of fear, suspicion and disdain. I would compliment them on their makeup or their hair, or I would ignore the painfully mixed metaphor and congratulate them on the insightful way they compared their soul to an endless dark hallway with a locked door at the end of it. In response they would either recoil as though I'd asked if they'd mind if I spat in their ear, or they would totally ignore me.

'It's because they've got no personality,' Wayne would tell me after yet another failed attempt to ingratiate myself with a purple-haired beauty.

'How could someone so gorgeous have no personality?'

'Too fuckin' easy.'

Deep down I agreed with Wayne, but whenever I saw a goth boy and a goth girl tucked away at the back of the pub, enmeshed in conversation, their pale white fingers entwined, their black-rimmed eyes staring into each other's, I would feel a pang of jealousy and think, 'Why him? Why not me? What's he got that I haven't?'

'Two cans of hairspray on his head and his own mascara,' was Wayne's standard reply.

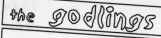

the godlings

Maitreya the Kid is what we call a Boddhisatva, an enlightened individual who chooses not to ascend to nirvana, but rather to stay here on the earthly plane.

Did you see my pizza, hanuman?

what kind was it?

tell me, maitreya. what was it that made you decide to stay here, rather than take your rightful place among the buddhas in heaven?

vegetarian with extra pineapple.

oh yeah. i ate it.

well, it WAS the pizza!

oopsie.

(sl.)

WEDNESDAY

My tyres buzz with last night's rain. Trees hang low over the footpaths, glistening green in the morning sun. Cool air fills my lungs as I suck in the smell of a freshly washed sky. Forty-nine Rae Street has a big parcel today. It won't fit in their tiny hole-in-the-wall mail slot, so I park my bike and, parcel in hand, peer behind the brick wall to see if it'll fit in the other side. I should just use a 'waiting for you at the post office' slip, but I'm distracted by the discovery that I've forgotten to bring chicken to work with me this morning.

Late nights do not agree with 5 a.m. starts. You'd think I'd have learned that after more than six months on the job. If I don't set myself up the night before so that all I have to do is climb into my clothes and stuff everything from my desk into my jacket pockets, the day will not go smoothly. And here I am, on a grey Wednesday morning, chickenless, cranky and about an hour later than I like to be. That's an extra hour for Satan to practise his repertoire of lunges, snatches and growls. All I've got to fend him off is a handful of tuna-flavoured cat biscuits. I'm not sure it's going to work. I don't think tuna tastes enough like mailman.

I cram the parcel into the hole in the wall. The wrapping tears slightly, but it stays in place. I push off and check the pannier—the next delivery is for Number 43. Down at the end of the street someone is standing outside their front fence. I grit my teeth and keep pedalling, hoping that I don't have mail for this guy. He's waiting there, staring intensely at me, a slight scowl on his face. Great. A complaint.

I give him an official Australia Post smile. He doesn't smile back. He's dressed sombrely—black denim jacket over black jeans. Black hair and neatly trimmed black goatee.

'Excuse me, but we have something that must be discussed,' he says.

I wait for him to continue, but he doesn't. There's a totally different expression on his face now, like he's just been punched in the guts. He starts mumbling to himself. I think I hear the word 'Helen', so I pull out his mail to see if there's a Helen or an 'H' on the address label. There isn't. This phone bill is addressed to Mr R. Thomson.

'I'm sorry?' I say.

'Natasha doesn't hold a candle to you,' he says.

Natasha? I thought we were talking about Helen. I lean forward to catch what he's saying. It sounds like . . . 'forgiveness? I forgive you'? And then maybe 'black dogs pounce'?

I straighten up. Black dogs pounce? Is he talking about Satan? How does he know about Satan? 'I'm sorry?'

'I'm sorry, Helen. Your eyes, they simply transfix me, representing as they do the randomness inflicted on us in this grim, grim world and the potential for infinite happiness that might skip past us at any moment like an empty supermarket bag easily snagged on the branches of a tree in winter. Your motorcycle seems a modest machine, but to me it will always be the courier of a kind and loving deity.'

I look to see if there's anyone else around, but there isn't. He's definitely talking to me. Brilliant. He's calling me Helen and he thinks I'm riding a motorbike. I liked it better when he was mumbling. Best to be extra polite when faced with strangers acting strange. I give him a 'well, there you go' smile and a 'shit happens' shrug and hand over the envelope.

'Just a phone bill today,' I offer, hoping that reality might jolt him out of the seizure, or whatever it is.

He takes the envelope with a dopey grin and drops to one knee. 'What can I present to you as a token of my love, Helen?'

I'm starting to wish I had that piece of chicken right now, so I could throw it at this guy. It's not enough that I have a homicidal Dober-man to deal with every morning? Now Mr Goatee has to fall in love with me?

'Umm, that's great, but I hardly know you,' I say, trying to improvise my way out of this. 'Look, I have to finish, umm, delivering the mail. Yeah. Have a nice day.' And I ride off.

He steps aside, still grinning that dopey grin. Two doors down, I take another look at him. He's at the gate, clutching the phone bill in both hands, staring into space, head tilted slightly upwards. I watch him for a moment, but he doesn't look poised to chase me down the street or anything. I sigh and make a mental note to keep an eye out for Mr Goatee from now on, and to leave Rae Street's deliveries until later, if I ever see him standing in wait for me again.

I scoot up Park Street, my tyres juddering over the uneven footpath, then make a right into Best, fritzing through a long shallow puddle. Only four more streets and then I can go home.

Earlier today at the delivery centre Wayne had been filling me in on his latest fling with a pretty young poet.

'You shoulda seen it, man. Well, maybe you shouldn't have. It was kind of private.'

'Shouldn't you have started loading by now?'

'Nah, after all the physical exertion last night, I reckon I should probably take it easy, know what I mean?'

'And how *is* Anthea?'

'It wasn't Anthea. We're having a few communication problems right now.'

'And nothing fixes a communication problem better than sleeping with someone else, hey?'

Wayne ignored me and continued ranting. 'Her name's Katie. She's great. She does these poems all about science and stuff. You know, stars and black holes and superstring theory?'

'Superstring theory? Like a piece of string with a little red cape?'

'Funny man. It's about parallel universes and stuff. Cutting-edge science. Anyway, last night she read this excellent poem about how they've just found nine more planets outside our solar system . . .'

'Wow. That's cool.'

'Yeah, so anyway I went up and talked to her after the open section, and we had some beers and got talking, and after they kicked us out we went back to my house because I had a bottle of bourbon stashed . . .'

I started packing my second bag. 'I can imagine.'

'But anyway, the point I was making was that the sex was great mainly because we kept stopping to read each other our poems.'

'So she tells you something clever about the nature of the universe and then you tell her something about being drunk at the Jamieson? That's pretty romantic, Wayne.'

'I better go pack,' he said and wandered over to his rack. I continued packing, marvelling at how it was that people like Wayne, who were admittedly charming—but also undeniably self-centred—managed to get so much sex.

Angsty is sitting on the fence at Number 72, one paw up, cleaning her chest. I stop in front of her and she pauses to look at me. She squeals.

'You sound like a baby,' I say, stuffing a bundle of mail into the slot in the fence. She squeals again. I squeal back. Then I scoop up a small handful of star-shaped biscuits from the special bag on my handlebars. Angsty sniffs the tips of my fingers and nibbles the powdery snacks from my palm, using her rough tongue to collect the last two. I dust my hand and scratch behind her ears, thinking about the nine new planets in the sky. I hope they've been given interesting names from mythology, not the obscure strings of numbers they give asteroids these days. Nothing worse than choosing XJ-104 instead of Clytemnestra or Ganesh. What if they found life on those planets? Would we call the new life-forms XJ-104ians? I'd much rather be a Clytemnestran or a Ganeshian than an XJ-104ian.

I give Angsty another scratch before standing on the pedals again.

The rain has kept most of the cats inside or under cover this morning, so it's pretty much just brake, reach, stuff, brake, reach, stuff until I'm parked outside Number 54, patting the chicken breast in my pocket and looking warily at Number 56's front gate.

I can't hear Satan. For a ridiculous Warner Brothers cartoon minute I think he must be lying in ambush for me. Then I remind myself that he's a big, dumb, vicious dog and as such isn't capable of coming up with a new plan to freak me out. But the silence is unnerving. By now I should have heard the ominous baritone growl. By now his moist and toothy snout should be visible, poking through the slats of the front gate. I push my bike forward cautiously until I'm right in front of the gate. Still nothing. I realise that I'm holding my breath and let out a gushy sigh. I peer through the gate, half expecting the bastard to jump up out of nowhere and make me shit my pants, but nothing happens. Instead I see Satan lying on his side on a beat-up couch on the veranda. I haven't seen the front yard of Number 56 for ages, because I'm always either flinching, flinging chicken or screaming past as fast as my bike will carry me. The lemon tree is covered in big yellow fruit, and the lawn could do with a water. The tranquillity of this scene is as unnerving as the silence.

I take advantage of the ceasefire and slip the mail in the mailbox. Satan still hasn't moved. He's probably all tuckered out from a big night of eating children and chasing bulldozers and now he's dreaming of dis-embowelling postal workers. I'm just about to push off when I have a premonition that something is wrong. I give the fence a sharp kick, but Satan doesn't react. Not even a twitch of his ears.

Before I know it I'm off my bike and through the front gate. I walk quickly and quietly up to Satan's recumbent form. A little man inside my head is screaming 'run, it's a trick, run for your life', but if this is a trick then I deserve to get bitten because this dog is not only a genius, he's a damn good actor as well. Those dogs they train to bark endorsements on TV ads have nothing on Satan. Hell, Lassie has nothing on Satan if this turns out to be a trick. If this turns out to be a trick I will buy a stack of one hundred *TV Weeks* and nominate him for the Readers' Choice section of the Logies.

I gently rest my hand on his flank. He doesn't move. He's cold to the touch. I notice what I think is a pool of vomit under his muzzle. Some of it is stuck to his lips. I watch him closely. He's not breathing. This is most definitely a dead dog.

I need a plan. I need to do something. I need to either run like buggery and pretend I never saw this, or ring the doorbell and let Satan's owner know what's going on. I'm tempted to run, I can't deny that that's my favourite option, but standing here, seeing the still form of my greatest nemesis brought low, I can't help but feel sorry for him. The Dalai Lama said that our enemies help us to define ourselves, and that we should love them for it, but I pretty much only ever hated this dog. Until now. Now I'm not so sure. The only thing I am sure of is that this little scenario is doing a real number on my head and I'm quoting the Dalai Lama and it's a dead dog, for god's sake, that's all, just a dead dog, so why am I freaking out so badly?

I close my eyes and take a deep breath. When I open my eyes again Satan is still there, his fur a little damp from the morning dew. I turn and walk up to the front door. My greatest nemesis brought low—where did that one come from? Mum was right, I definitely read too many comics when I was younger. I press the doorbell. I hear soft footsteps, then the door opens to reveal a four-and-a-half-foot-tall elderly woman. According to the envelope I've just stuffed in her mailbox, this must be Mrs Fraser. Mrs A. Fraser, known in certain circles as she-who-breeds-monsters-and-who-further-more-ignores-complaints-about-said-monsters-attacking-official-represent-atives-of-Australia-Post. In real life she doesn't look much like a monster-breeder. She's wearing a lavender-grey cardigan pulled close around her shoulders. Her hair is silvery white. She'd make a great poster girl for lovely old ladies everywhere. She looks up at me with steel-grey eyes.

'Yea?' Her accent is broadly Scottish.

I smile in what I hope is a confidence-inspiring manner. 'Um, hi. I'm the guy who delivers your mail.' I'm trying to sound calm and respectful, but I'm coming across as nervous and stupid.

'Yea?'

'Well, I was just putting your mail in the box.'

She peers around me, looking to see what's wrong with the box, I suppose, and then squints back up at me.

'Yea?'

I'm getting a big Robbie Coltrane vibe. I look down, trying not to smile at the vision of Robbie dressed as a nun that's just popped into my head. This is not a smiling occasion.

'Well, I noticed that there was something wrong with your dog . . .'

She leans out of the doorway, and when she sees Satan lying on the couch she cries out, pushes past me, and runs over to her dog's body. 'Gavin! Mah wee bebeh! What's wrong wi' ye?'

Gavin? What kind of a name for a dog is 'Gavin'? I suppose it's Scottish-sounding. Maybe she named him after her husband.

Mrs Fraser rests her hand under Satan's—Gavin's—muzzle and bends down, lifting his face to hers. There's no response. Obviously. I stare help-lessly as she rests her head against Satan's—that is to say, Gavin's—face and starts to cry.

The sound of her crying snaps me out of it and I take a step forward. 'If there's anything I can do to help . . .'

She straightens up. Her face is red, but she doesn't look sad. She looks pissed off. 'YOU did this to him!' she screams.

I'm stunned. I frown. I open my mouth to say something, but all that comes out is a meek yelp. 'What?'

She takes a step towards me and points a bony finger. 'I know what you did! You HATED mah bebeh! I've seen you feed him in the mornings, always ruining his appetite for lunch! But that wasn't enough for ye, was it? No, OH no! Ye had to go further. YOU POISONED HIM WITH YOUR CHICKEN! YOU KILLED MAH BEBEH!'

I back away, off the veranda and down the garden path. Lunch? She fed him lunch? What did she feed him? Ex-politicians? Dole bludgers?

She follows, shaking her fist at me. 'YOU MURDERED HIM! MURDERER! MURDERER!'

This woman has officially moved beyond distraught and into insane. I turn around, jump the gate and scramble onto my bike. 'Look, I know this must be a difficult time for you right now, but I swear I just found him like that,' I say, adopting what I hope is a conciliatory tone.

'LIAR!' She's standing at her gate now. Her face is bright pink and she's spitting a little when she yells.

I flinch and pedal away.

'YOU HAVEN'T HEARD THE LAST OF THIS!' she screams at me.

I turn to see her standing out the front of her place, shaking her little fist in the air.

I drop mail at Number 42, then deliver bundles to Numbers 40 through 34 and 30 through 20. I scoot straight past Number 16, ignoring Malkin, who is perched on top of the high fence, waiting for me, and then I turn right, almost collecting a jogger as I look back one last time to see Mrs Fraser still outside her gate. I decide to leave the odd numbers on Best Street for later. Grief does strange things to people, I tell myself, figuring that the situation will probably settle back to normal by tomorrow morning. Maybe I'll visit her again next week, when she's had time to calm down, and I can explain myself then.

I pull back into the delivery centre at about one o'clock. Wayne's still out on his run. I'm in the process of writing him a note along the lines of 'give us a call we should do beer tonight' when Sully taps me on the shoulder.

'Boss wants to see you in his office when you're done.'

'Any idea what it's about?'

Sully shakes his head. 'Didn't say. What do you reckon?'

I think for a moment. 'Probably needs a timesheet for last week. He's always bloody losing them.'

Sully nods and wanders off to the canteen.

David's got his solemn face on. This isn't about the timesheet. This is something else. I run through all the things I've done lately that might be construed as inappropriate for an Australia Post employee. I can think of a few that would make him cranky, but none that he would have found out about. Whatever it is, I can tell I'm in deep shit.

'I had a phone call from a Mrs Abigail Fraser this morning. A complaint.'

Abigail. The A is for Abigail. Instinctively I play it innocent. 'The complaint was about me?'

David looks down at a piece of paper resting on his desk. 'Mrs Fraser was very distraught, but she managed to explain to me that she believes that you, Steven, are responsible for the death of her dog.' He looks up at me, expecting a response.

I take a deep breath. 'Ah, yeah. That. Well, you see, David, what happened was I saw her dog lying on the veranda and it didn't look well, so I figured something was wrong because it's usually not lying there on the veranda. It's usually trying to bite off my fingers, actually, as you would know from the series of complaints that I've brought to your attention, complaints that, I might point out, have been ineffectual in dealing with the situation. So I went inside the yard to see if it was okay, and it wasn't. It was dead. But I didn't kill it.'

David maintains his poker face and continues. 'Mrs Fraser doesn't see it that way. In fact, Mrs Fraser claims that you have been feeding her dog drugged meat for months now, and that this is what killed her dog.'

Drugged meat? What kind of idiot would feed a dog drugged meat? Actually, it's not such a bad idea. A bit of Rohypnol in the chicken would have kept Satan quiet for longer—why didn't I think of that? Because it's a stupid idea, that's why.

'Why would I want to kill her dog? Why would I want to kill anyone's dog?'

'Have you been feeding her dog, Steven?'

I pause for a moment and feel myself going red. 'Um, well . . . okay, yes. I've been throwing chicken breasts over the fence, but only so that it would be distracted long enough for me to get the mail into the mailbox, because I've told you about the problem with Mrs Fraser's dog a few times now and nothing ever happened, except I lost a scarf one time, but I never drugged the meat or anything, that would be stupid.' I smile a smile that is intended to be disarming.

'Well, stupid or not, it's Mrs Fraser's contention.'

'I didn't kill the dog, David.'

David leans across the desk, his hands clasped in front of him. He leans so close that I can smell the rubber-band smell on his hands. 'I don't think you did kill that dog, Steven, but I am concerned that you were in violation of conventions that we expect everyone to observe here.' He leans back in his chair. 'Your job is to deliver mail, Steven. Nothing more. You are not supposed to fraternise with the customers' pets.'

'But it was trying to take my throat out. What else could I do? And anyway, I wasn't "fraternising". You can't "fraternise" with hell-hounds.'

'I'm not referring solely to this particular incident, Steven. I'm referring also to the containers of cat biscuits that you carry on your handlebars.'

Busted. How did he know about that? I grit my teeth and keep quiet.

'You must understand that by engaging in these activities you open Australia Post up to potential legal consequences, as is highlighted by today's incident. Australia Post is liable for any damage that you may cause in the carrying out of your duties. Australia Post would have to compensate anyone who could prove that you had hurt their pet.'

'I was only being friendly.' The words hang lamely in the air just above David's desk.

'It's not your job to be friendly to cats, Steven. It's your job to deliver mail. What you have done is irresponsible and careless. I've spoken to upper management about this incident. Fortunately we were able to placate Mrs Fraser and convince her not to press charges against the company or yourself.'

Charges? This is getting out of hand. I figure I might as well save my energy, back down, and apologise, especially since David isn't listening to my side of the story anyway. 'I'm really sorry, David. I didn't realise I was causing so much trouble. It'll never happen again.'

David nods his head slightly. 'Be that as it may, I'm afraid we are going to have to discipline you over this matter.'

Again I grit my teeth, trying to look humble rather than pissed off.

David sighs deeply. 'As of tomorrow you will be reassigned to another run. Obviously you can't continue to deliver mail to Mrs Fraser, so upper management and I have decided to move you to Aki Johnston's run. Aki will swap with you tomorrow.'

'Aki's run? But that's all the way over in Northcote!' I wince at the whiny tone in my voice.

'Yes.'

'And it's twice as long as the one I'm doing now!' The whiny tone is still there. I clear my throat.

'I'm aware of that, Steven.'

'And it's all bloody hills!' I manage to sound a little more assertive this time, but only a little.

'Think yourself lucky, Steven. We could have transferred you to another DC entirely. We can do that, you know. We're actually being generous. Just don't push your luck.'

I slump forward, resting my head in my hand and my elbows on the desk. 'I don't suppose there's any way I could appeal this?' I ask. The whiny tone is back.

'No, Steven. There isn't.'

'Fine,' I say, managing to level my voice out to a resigned monotone. 'I guess that's it then.'

David does his best impersonation of a sympathetic person. 'I'm sorry, Steven. You left us no choice. Maybe you'll think twice before putting us in such a precarious position again.'

I stand up to leave the office. David stands as well. 'Thank you, Steven. I'm glad we could have this chat.'

I shut his office door without replying.

Back at the bike rack I unhook the pannier bags and carry them over to my cubicle. Sully raises his eyebrows by way of asking what went on.

'He fuckin' moved me to Aki's run.' On the 'fuckin'' I toss the bags into the corner of the desk. Yes, I am one cranky mailman right now.

Sully's eyebrows climb even higher up his ample forehead and he whistles softly. 'How come?'

'It's a long story, Sully. I'll tell you tomorrow.'

I grab my bike from the back of the shed and hit the road, replaying the meeting in my head and swearing quietly as I work out my anger on the pedals. I get home in record time.

The window of the pub lounge has posters sticky-taped to the glass. I recognise some of the names, but nothing really catches my fancy. I shoulder the heavy side-door open. It's fuggy inside. Warm. Cosy. I scan for familiar faces, then walk up to the bar. There's a spare stool just near the cash register, next to a girl wearing a black skivvy underneath a purple lace top. I sit down next to her and smile. She rolls her black-rimmed eyes, then stands up and sashays into the band area, taking her long fake-fur coat and glass of red wine with her. I watch her wiggle over to the darkest corner in the pub, then I shrug out of my jacket and check out the rest of the crowd.

Not many people out tonight, but it's only Wednesday. Wednesday, I think to myself. Three days into the week and everything's gone to shit. Tomorrow morning I start on Aki's run, and Aki starts on mine. Tomorrow morning I introduce my calf muscles to Rucker's Hill and the steep stretch up Wilson Street. I've had it far too easy, cruising the flats of East Brunswick and North Fitzroy. Now I'll have to get fit. I'm not looking forward to it. Going to miss all my cat buddies, too.

'Hey, babe!' Gina taps my shoulder and gives me a quick hug before walking around behind the bar and handing me a beer. She stacks dirty glasses into a tray.

'Hey.'

'That bad, huh?' She can tell from my face that something's up.

I nod and start peeling the label off my beer. 'Totally shitful day. I got relocated to a different run.'

'What? Can they do that?'

I shrug. 'Pretty much. They didn't fire me or anything. It's the same job, same wages, same duties. Just a different run.'

'Hang on a sec,' she says, and serves a guy on the other side of the bar. 'So what happened?'

I take a deep breath and relate this morning's events, painfully aware that it sounds like a poorly written black comedy.

When I'm done Gina just stands there, head cocked to one side, frowning. 'There's got to be something we can do to get your run back,' she says. 'Let me think about this for a while.'

I suck the remains of my beer and place the empty back on the bar. I'm about to point out that technically I was in the wrong, but I know that look. She's getting an Idea. There's no stopping her when she gets an Idea. It's best just to go along with her. Sometimes it's even fun.

⏪

I first met Gina when I was at university. I was working at a call centre three evenings a week, asking the same stupid questions to different uninterested people fifty to a hundred times a night so that I could afford to pay my rent. Gina was my shift manager. She assigned the slabs of phone numbers we had to trawl through.

We became friends when we discovered a mutual appreciation of bad American television. I was in the kitchenette making myself a coffee, whistling the theme song from *The Greatest American Hero*.

'I used to watch that show when I was little,' she said.

'Me too. My dad even bought the theme song on single. We used to play it all the time. They don't make shows like that any more.'

'Thank god for that, hey?'

'I thought my dad *was* the Greatest American Hero.'

'What?'

'Yeah, he had blond curly hair just like him, and he used to wear red pyjamas in bed.'

'A dead giveaway.'

'And when I asked him if it was true, he'd just smirk and tell me that a good superhero never reveals his secret identity.'

'What was that actor's name?'

'No idea.'

'I wonder what he's up to these days.'

'I don't.'

We got to talking about all those dreadful eighties shows we vaguely remembered from our childhoods, like the *A-Team, Remington Steele, The Fall Guy* and *Who's The Boss?* Gina's favourite was *Murder, She Wrote*, the one about Jessica Fletcher, the lady crime novelist who solves murder mysteries in her spare time. Gina used to sit up past her bedtime, snuggled in her mother's lap, not really understanding what was going on, but enraptured all the same.

The premise of the show is that Jessica Fletcher has written so many murder mystery novels that she has a unique understanding of how a murderer's mind works, and can solve crimes better than the police. Every week she somehow finds herself involved in a murder case, and through careful investigation and reliance on her crime-novelist hunches she uncovers the truth and brings the perpetrators to justice. Nobody ever thinks to ask why this eccentric crime novelist is coincidentally at the scene of a murder every single week.

Gina loved Jessica Fletcher, loved the way she second-guessed the bad guys, loved the way she made the cops look like idiots, and especially loved the smug-yet-humble demeanour that she adopted when revealing who the killer really was.

'She's some feisty chick. She's got the moves, she knows what's going on. Jessica Fletcher is my hero.'

'She's the murderer.'

'Don't ever let Mum hear you say that, Steven. Bad-mouth Jessica, and you're history.'

Now, I'm all for lionising the stars of crappy American TV. I love to lampoon the poorly written scripts, the hack actors, the plodding moralistic values 'hidden' in the subtext of these shows. But Gina's affection for *Murder, She Wrote* seems to go further than simple irony. It's a little disturbing. Sometimes I wonder if there *is* an ironic component to her love of the show. But even when Gina's at her most twisted, I love being around her because it's invariably more entertaining than not being around her.

At the call centre we would email Internet gossip to each other, about the actors from various US schlock-TV shows: what David Hasselhoff was up to these days, rumours of a *Hart to Hart* reunion special, cinematic cameo appearances by the guy who played Howling Mad Murdock. One time, Gina even sent me pictures of the cast of *The Greatest American Hero* with my face pasted over all of theirs. After work we'd go out drinking, watch 24-hour science fiction movie marathons and memorise the dumbest lines to scream at each other in the pub, bitch about the zombies we worked with at the call centre and swap stories about the minefields that were our love lives.

It was inevitable that our bonding over trash culture would set us up as some kind of two-person clique at work, and also inevitable that our workmates would come to think of us as 'those two loud weirdoes'. We expected such a reaction, and we revelled in it. What we didn't anticipate was that our 'misuse of company technology' (translation: logging into the TrashTeevee message board an average of fifteen times a day) would get us fired.

The night of our last shift, Gina and I sent a company-wide spam email with a big picture of David Hasselhoff smiling his best *Knight Rider* smile as he perched on the bonnet of K.I.T.T., his sentient crime-fighting car. To accompany the picture we had composed a farewell message.

Your computer has been infected by the Knight Rider virus!! This virus is EXTREMELY DANGEROUS!!! It transforms your hard-drive into a sentient, crime-fighting robot with flashing red eyes and a patronising English accent! It transforms the user into a curly-haired 80s bohunk with a fetish for leather pants!!! The only cure is to watch seasons one through five of Baywatch *sequentially, though the user runs the risk of turning into a curly-haired 90s bohunk with a fetish for red Speedos!!!! BEWARE!!!!!*

Neither of us has worked in the telemarketing industry since. Gina scored herself a sweet gig tending bar at the Empress, and I fell back into the generous arms of Austudy for the remainder of my degree.

So in return for the joys of sharing Gina's company and having her include me in her outlandish schemes, which can only be described as 'cocka-mamie', I pretend not to be disturbed by the giant poster of Jessica Fletcher that is the focal point of Gina's lounge room. I turn a blind eye to the bookshelf filled with videotaped episodes of *Murder, She Wrote* that her mother actually listed tape by tape on her household insurance form. I join Gina and her mother for their *M,SW* marathon parties, watching back-to-back episodes until I fall asleep on the couch, with the two of them sitting up well into the morning, calling out encouragement to their on-screen heroine.

   'Attagirl, Jess! You tell that nosey Amos Tupper to keep his opinions to himself!'

   'You tell him, Mum.'

But there's one thing I cannot tolerate. One thing about the show that drives me absolutely out of my skull.

That goddamn comma.

'What the hell is it doing there?' I once asked Gina.

'I don't see the problem,' she countered.

'It's grammatically incorrect! It's not a bloody sentence! It makes no sense!'

'What? It's perfectly clear. Murder, she wrote. She's a mystery writer. She writes murder novels. See?'

'No, I don't see. If that was what you were trying to get across, then you'd write "she wrote murder", or something.'

'"She wrote murder" sounds dumb.'

'So does "Murder, she wrote"! At least you could put quote marks in there. If it said "Quote, Murder, comma, unquote, She Wrote", then that would at least be grammatically correct. I could see that. I could understand what was going on there.'

'Calm down, boy. It's just a television show.'

I raised my eyebrows and motioned to the four-foot tall photograph behind us, smiling into the lounge room like a cross between Chairman Mao and Ronald McDonald.

'Okay, okay, so it's not just a television show,' Gina admitted. 'But it's not worth getting all messed up over a comma. You're not going to change anything now. They stopped making it years ago. It's history now. Murder. Comma. She. Wrote.'

I sighed in exasperation and settled back into the couch. On screen, Jessica was explaining her latest hunch to a room of assembled guests.

Gina poked me in the ribs. 'You get worked up over the smallest things, mate.'

'It's a matter of principle.'

She kissed me on the cheek and went into the kitchen to grab another couple of beers. I stuck my tongue out while her back was turned.

A week after the comma conversation Gina had turned up on my doorstep at around ten-thirty at night.

'Hey,' I said. 'I was just getting ready for bed.'

She was dressed in a black Bonds long-sleeved T-shirt and a pair of black jeans.

'I've got a plan.'

I stood in the doorway, waiting for an elaboration.

'You have to get changed,' she said. 'Into black clothes. We're on a mission.'

Gina followed me up to my room. She had her hands tucked behind her back, and she was grinning.

'What?' I asked.

She thrust a stack of A4 sheets at me.

'Your mission, should you choose to accept it.'

I flipped through the stack. They were all the same.

'You must have some black clothes in here somewhere,' she said, rummaging around in my wardrobe.

'There's a pair of jeans in the bottom cupboard, and I think my black jumper's in the lounge.'

'I'll go grab it,' she said.

I took a closer look at the pages Gina had handed me.

We represent Citizens for Correct Grammar In Public Spaces (CCGIPS). Your place of business is in contravention of the prime directive of our organisation. The signage that you currently display incorrectly utilises apostrophes. We request that you amend your signage to bring it in line with the standards set and observed by the Australian Government Printing Service (AGPS), the recognised authority in matters of grammar usage and style in Australia.

You have two weeks to comply. If you have not complied by the end of this two-week period, further steps will be taken.

Yours sincerely
Jessica Fletcher
(secretary, CCGIPS)

—Guidelines follow—

Apostrophe:

6.162 The principal use of the apostrophe, normally followed or preceded by s, is to indicate possession (also indicated by using the preposition of):

> the horse's mouth (= the mouth of the horse)
> the horses' mouths (= the mouths of the horses)

6.163 The apostrophe is needed to indicate possession with nouns only; the pronouns hers, its, theirs and yours are already possessive and do not need the apostrophe. It's means 'it is', while its means 'belonging to it'.

(For further information on the use of apostrophes, please refer to the Style Manual for Authors, Editors and Printers, *published by the Australian Government Printing Service.)*

Gina came back with my black jumper tucked under her arm.

'What's this?' I asked.

'Our constitution.'

'But I was just going to bed.'

'And now you're not. We've got work to do.'

'Don't you have a date tonight?'

'Don't you?'

I grabbed the jumper and pulled it over my head, then stared at her for a moment.

'What?'

'I need to get changed.'

'I've seen my brothers naked, you know. It's not like you've got anything I haven't seen before.'

'You haven't got any brothers.'

'Oh. Well, I'm sure they were *somebody's* brothers . . .'

'Get out, dickhead.'

'Are you this coy around other girls?'

I stared Gina down and she left the room. I slid out of my blue jeans and into the black. 'Want to clue me in?' I called.

Gina came back to watch me dig out my old black Converse boots. 'I got to thinking about the whole comma thing, and I felt sorry for you, Steven. It must be hard to live in a world that so frequently abuses punctuation.'

'It's torture.'

'Well, I came up with a plan. We can't do anything about Jessica's comma now, but we *can* take action on a local level. We're going out onto the streets and we're going to paste these notices on the windows of any shops that have the temerity to blatantly and publicly contradict the rules of good grammar.'

'We're going to what?'

'You heard.'

'Yeah, but I thought I mightn't've.'

'You heard.'

'Vandalism? Aren't we a little bit old to embark on a life of petty crime?'

'It's never too late. Besides, this is vandalism for a higher cause.'

The back seat of Gina's car was covered with what looked like the standard beginner's postering kit: papers, brushes and a bucket half-filled with grey gluggy stuff.

'What's in the bucket?' I asked.

'Rice flour and water. The best postering glue there is. Cooked it up an hour ago.'

I stuck a finger into the gunk. It was still warm. 'Thought of everything, haven't we?'

'Let's start out on High Street. Bound to be a couple of likely candidates for a pasting up that way.'

'I know just the one,' I said. I'd caught a tram past the second-hand furniture store just the other week and had stared aghast at its blatant grammatical infringement. Painted in fluorescent pink capital letters outlined in bright yellow was the phrase '1000's of BARGAINS INSIDE!!'. At the time I had contemplated tossing a rock through the window on my way back, but now I had a much more educational and constructive alternative.

'Totally inappropriate,' mumbled Gina as she stepped out of the car. I stood silently on the kerb, clutching the stack of leaflets. Gina came up beside me, bucket in hand, and we stood in front of the offending window to consider our approach.

'I'll glue if you keep a lookout,' she said. 'We can swap later.'

I nodded and passed her a pamphlet. She slapped it on top of the offending number, and painted a liberal amount of paste over it. I leaned against the car, glancing around. Only a few other cars were parked on the street. A block or so towards Separation Street, people were hanging around outside the pool hall. The Number 86 tram whispered past on its way into the city. A quiet week-night in Northcote.

Gina stepped back to admire her handiwork. 'That oughta learn 'em.'

The paste had covered the entire pamphlet in a greyish white sludge, obscuring the text.

'That stuff dries clear, right?' I asked.

'You bet. Clear and immovable. Let's find another one.'

We didn't have to look far. Two blocks south, the front window of Northcote Whitegoods King announced: 'Fridge's, Washer's & Dryer's DRAS-TICALLY REDUCED'. I clucked my tongue in disapproval and set to work.

'Hey, check this out,' said Gina. She was pointing to a spot on the wall between Whitegoods King and the real estate agency next door. Stuck at about head-height was a round sticker with a stylised picture of a man lifting a box, using the workplace-safety-endorsed bend-from-the-knees method. Underneath him, white on black, was the legend, 'THIS IS A HEAVY PRODUCT'.

'He gets everywhere, doesn't he?' I said.

'Yeah,' said Gina. 'I was out Werribee way last week and I saw one stuck up on the sign at Laverton Station.'

'What the hell were you doing way out at Werribee?'

'Oh, a friend of Cameron's was getting married in the mansion.'

'The *mansion*?'

'Yeah. Werribee Mansion. Big reception centre. You don't get out of the inner city much, do you?'

'Am I missing anything?'

'Not really, no.'

'So how was it?'

'Okay, except we broke up during the reception. I had to leave a bit earlier than planned.'

'Did you dump or did he?'

'Me, stupid. I saw him with all his old school mates and married friends and parents and stuff and . . . I dunno, I just realised that I didn't like him as much as I thought. All the dumb in-jokes just kind of sealed the deal for me.'

'Ah.'

'I figured it would be best to do it then, because he had his friends there to help him get over it. A good supportive environment.'

'Have I met Cameron?'

'Yeah—he was the guy I was with at the pub last week.'

'Blond? He seemed nice.'

'He was. Is.'

We both stared at the sticker in silence.

'So what do you reckon it means?' I asked.

'Not much, really. We'd only been going out for a month. We just didn't click.'

'Not Cameron, idiot. The sticker.'

'Oh. Dunno. But I'd love to know who's doing it.'

'Maybe it's more than one person.'

'Mmm.' Gina tried to peel the sticker from the wall with her thumbnail. She managed to lift one end free, but it tore when she pulled harder. 'How many do you reckon we'll spot tonight?'

'Northcote? It's kind of his territory. Um—ten?'

'Or *her* territory. Fifteen.'

'You're on.'

I collected the bucket and loaded it onto the back seat, spilling a little on my jeans. We pulled out onto High Street and headed north.

We dealt with fourteen grammar infringements that night, covering the suburbs of Northcote and Thornbury with tokens of our pedantic wrath. We both underestimated the number of Heavy Product stickers, spotting more than twenty on bus stops, pub frontages and shop doorways all the way from Northcote to Preston. By the time we got back to my place it was 2 a.m., and we were spattered with paste. My fingers stuck together every time I made a fist.

'Next time we bring a sponge and some water,' I said.

'Hey, it's a dirty job but someone's got to do it.' Gina kept the motor running while I got out of the car. 'You do realise, Steven, that your obsession with punctuation could be interpreted as a particularly Anglocentric attitude, don't you?'

'I guess.' I hadn't thought of it like that. 'I was looking at it more as an expression of smugness and superiority.'

'Well, that's okay then.'

I watched her pull up at the corner and indicate left. I turned and headed inside, peeling a torn corner of one of the posters from the bottom of my boot as I nudged the door open.

I stare at the muted TV in the pub, picking at the label on my empty beer bottle. It's one of those gritty Australian cop dramas with semi-famous film actors in it. Two tough-looking guys are pinning a weedy kid up against a garage roller-door. The camera keeps cutting between the kid's face and the blond cop's face, which is all screwed up and red from being so pissed off and tough.

Someone taps me on the shoulder. 'G'day, mate.' It's Wayne.

'How you goin'?'

'Pretty good, yeah. Beer?' He turns to the bar and rests his elbows on the damp bar-towel. 'Heard you had a bit of an altercation with a client today. Whole bloody shed's talking about it.'

'Satan died today. His owner thinks I killed him.'

'Satan's dead? How Nietzschean.'

'Not funny.'

'A bit obvious. Sorry. Did you kill him?'

'Fuck you, Wayne.' I take a big slug of beer. 'It was your bloody idea to use the chicken in the first place.'

'Well, it worked up until now, didn't it? In fact, you could say it's still working.'

Satan wasn't always a feature of my run. Back in the early days of my postal career, letters addressed to 56 Best Street had the name Salvatore Cartolina on them. I never met Salvatore, or any of his pets. Interactions with 56 Best were as uneventful as any mail-delivery interaction could be. Things changed when Mrs A. (A is for Abigail) Fraser moved in. Number 56 quickly became the highest and pointiest spike on the graph of dog-bite-related tension in my life. A hot spot of adrenal activity, leaving a psychic trace with enough intensity to draw remote-viewers from all over the astral plane, who, when woken by their supervisors, could only say, 'Teeth . . . big, slimy teeth . . .' and then ask to be relieved of duty.

My first encounter with Satan was typical of the way things were to go.

I had been off work a week, after a dickhead in a minivan tried to reverse over me. On my first day back at the depot I noticed the change of name on the mail going to Number 56, but I didn't think anything of it until I was on the run. I was just sliding the mail into the box when the whole gate crashed forward onto its frame. I made one of those 'ah-bah-AHH' noises you make when a friend jumps out at you from behind a doorway because they think it'd be funny to see you have a heart attack, and I fell over sideways, taking my bike with me. I lay on the footpath, dazed. One pedal was digging into my calf, and my elbow was shredded. I couldn't focus on either, though, because a particular noise was taking up the entire local sensory environment. An angry wolf was operating some kind of industrial machinery right in front of me. I opened my eyes and twisted around onto my back, scraping more skin off my calf. First day back at work after falling off my bike and what do I do? Fall off my bike. Brilliant.

Behind the gate was a dark form, about five feet tall. Slowly the growling resolved into the sound of a very big, very angry Doberman pinscher, with its front paws up against the gate, barking very loudly at me. I swore and extricated myself from my bike. Fucking attack dogs, I thought. Big bully-dogs trained by small-dicked bully-owners, acting all tough while they're safe on their side of the fence.

I stood up shakily and propped the bike on its kickstand. The mail for Number 56 was lying on the ground, one end tucked under the gate. I bent to pick it up. The dog dropped onto all fours, and thrust its snout between the gate and the ground, snapping wildly at my fingers. I pulled my arm back. The dog stayed where it was, two fangs poking out from under its top lip, growling like an idling motorcycle.

Okay, so maybe there was more than just simple showing off involved with this dog. I couldn't risk trying to get the mail back, with that mean bastard's snout resting right on it, but I wasn't supposed to leave it there.

Regulations state that if there's a mailbox provided by the customer, we have to use it. That mail had to go in the box. I stepped back to give myself room and kicked at the snout, hoping to call the dog's bluff and send it yapping around to the backyard. I didn't expect to make contact. But instead of yelping and retreating, the dog simply opened its jaws, still growling, and caught the toe of my boot in its mouth. I tried to pull free. I tripped and hit the ground again, feeling the dog's teeth close over my toes. Logically, I knew it couldn't bite through my steel-caps, but I was beyond logic. Yelping, I yanked hard and managed to get my toe free. The dog clamped its jaws shut again, this time over the loop in my bootlace.

For a stunned second I felt myself being pulled underneath the gate. I screamed and twisted onto my stomach. With one leg, I pushed against the footpath, and with the other I strained against the dog's entire weight. The laces cut into my foot as they tightened. I considered undoing the laces and letting the dog keep the boot, but there was no way I was putting my hands any closer to that mouth.

I heard a growl of what sounded like triumph. I closed my eyes. It would only take a moment for the bastard to realise that a much better grip could be had by sinking his teeth directly into my ankle. I gave one last yank, praying that, in blatant contradiction to the way it had been con-structed, my boot would simply slip off, and suddenly the force I was acting against was gone. I slammed headfirst into the rear wheel of my bike, knocking it into the gutter. My shoelace had snapped.

I scrambled to my feet, and there was the dog up against the fence again, barking maniacally. I closed my eyes for a moment and let out a deep breath before rescuing my bike, stuffing the scattered mail back into my pannier, and riding off with an attempt at dignity, ignoring the slamming of the gate against its frame and the in-direct-contravention-of-the-rules mail lying shredded on the footpath. My front wheel squealed plaintively as it rubbed its buckled rim against the fork. I knew exactly how it felt.

Back at the depot I dumped my bike, chucked the bags on my desk and limped over to the kitchen. I rummaged around the first-aid cabinet, pulled out some disinfectant and rolled my jeans up to inspect the damage. My right knee was tender, but it was only bruised. I winced as I dabbed Dettol onto the scratch on my calf.

'Take a tumble, did we?' Wayne stood in the doorway, watching me stick a bandaid over my wound.

'Some kind of wolf moved in on my run.'

Wayne took a carton of milk from the fridge and began sucking on the spout. A little milk ran down his chin and along the line of his throat. He gasped, satisfied, and shook the carton. It sounded like there was only a trickle in there, but he stuck it back in the fridge anyway. I started dabbing Dettol on my elbow.

'Gave you a bit of a fright, eh?'

'Yeah. A bit.'

'What kind of dog?'

'Doberman. Big. Black. Teeth. I swear it tried to jump through the fucking gate.'

'That'd be Satan, then.'

I looked up. 'Satan?'

'Yeah, Sully mentioned a big bastard on your run, but I told him you were almost one hundred per cent pussycat territory. We worked out it must be the new owner's or something.'

'You KNEW about it? And you didn't say anything?'

'I forgot. I figured Sully'd tell you.'

'I haven't seen him since I got back.'

'He's off on his run now. He got in late.'

'Satan. That kind of fits.'

'It was Sully's idea. Apparently it nearly got his fingers.'

I headed for David's office.

'Did Sully tell you about the new customer on my run? The one with the problem dog?'

'Yes, he did, and I contacted the customer in question later that day. Mrs Fraser promised that she would take appropriate precautions.'

'Well, the dog in question nearly had my foot for breakfast this morning. I don't know what precautions she's taking, but they're not working.' I rolled up my sleeve and pointed at my freshly bandaided elbow.

'It bit you on the elbow?'

I paused. 'No, it jumped out at me and I fell off my bike.'

David raised his eyebrows and smirked. 'Ah. I see.'

I waited for a better response.

David looked down at his desk and shuffled some papers. 'Well, I'll call Mrs Fraser again and raise the matter with her.'

He'd better not raise anything with Satan, I thought. Anything raised in that monster's direction would get bitten off.

The next afternoon I was back in David's office.

'It ate the mail.'

'I'm sorry?' David asked.

'You heard me. The dog ate the mail!'

'This would be the dog at . . .' He shuffled a few papers on the top of his desk.' . . . Number 56 Best Street, yes?'

'Uh-huh.'

'Now, when you say it ate the mail . . .'

'It wedged its head through the gate, snatched the mail out of my hand and went for my fingers. When I pulled back, it bent down and tore the mail into tiny little pieces!'

'Ah. I'm not sure what I can do, Steven. I've contacted Mrs Fraser since we last spoke, and she promised me she would deal with the situation.'

'Well, she bloody hasn't, and I'm not taking any responsibility if she has to wait until the dog takes a dump before I can deliver her mail.'

'Calm down, Steven.'

'I AM calm!'

'Take a seat. Now, you understand, don't you, that when you came on board with Australia Post you signed an agreement with us to fulfil the duties of your job description?'

I sat down. 'Yeah, but there wasn't anything about having to deal with the bad guy from "Little Red Riding Hood"!'

'And you do understand that failing to deliver Mrs Fraser's mail in a reasonable condition and in a reasonable location constitutes action that warrants disciplinary procedures?'

I sighed. 'Yes, but . . .'

'Then I trust that this matter is settled. I will, once again, on your behalf, express your concerns to Mrs Fraser. And you will continue to see that her mail is delivered—'

'In a reasonable condition and in a reasonable location. I get it.'

'I'm glad.' David smiled and went back to paper-shuffling.

'He doesn't give a shit,' I said to Wayne. 'I can't believe he was ever out there. Doesn't have a clue what we do, does he?'

'No, mate. That's why he's management and you're a shit-kicking postie.'

'Meanwhile, I still have to deal with Satan.'

We were sitting opposite each other at the corner milk bar, which had somehow found room to wedge a small table and four chairs over by the chips display, so that it could justify the words 'and cafe' painted on the window. Wayne and I usually had our after-work bitch sessions there when we knocked off at the same time.

'You could have him shot,' Wayne offered.

'Could be a she.'

'Wouldn't matter to the bullet,' Wayne winked.

'Don't tempt me.'

Wayne sipped at the remains of his coffee.

'You should've seen it, mate. It broke one of the slats and shoved its head fully outside the gate. I got dog-drool on my fingers.'

'There's got to be a way around it,' mused Wayne. 'We just have to work out what it is.'

'Chicken,' Wayne said to me the next morning.

'You are,' I replied.

'Nah, mate. Give the dog chicken.'

I paused for a moment and set the stack of envelopes down in front of my rack. 'Give the dog chicken.'

'Yeah. Throw a piece of chicken fillet over the fence, and while the fucker's off after it, stick the mail in the box. By the time it gets back, you're four houses down and away.'

'You want me to feed the fucker? *Reward* it for trying to take a piece out of me? That's brilliant, Wayne. Brilliant.'

'It'd work though,' he insisted.

'Yeah, as an appetiser.'

It only took a day for me to come around to Wayne's idea. Having the hem of my trousers shredded for the third time in a month sealed it. That night I dropped in on my local supermarket and picked up a full tray of chicken breast fillets. The next morning I halved one, wrapped it in Gladwrap, and stuffed it in my jacket pocket.

And so began the ritual of flinging a damp lump of chicken breast as high and far over the fence of Number 56 as I could. From the first day of execution, the plan went perfectly. Satan would trot over to the meat, and by the time he had choked it down I would be houses away.

That first night, Gina and Wayne came over for pizza and videos, and when I told them how Satan had been successfully vanquished, they insisted that we celebrate with pizza and a five-dollar bottle of champagne. The combination of cheap, fizzy booze and stodgy, salty cheese left us in a state of silent contentment as we half-watched and half-dozed our way through some crap science fiction film and chased it down with an episode of *Murder, She Wrote* that Gina 'just happened' to bring along. It was a freaky episode about someone using a poison spray to kill a person in a confessional. Wayne and I laughed when we realised that one of the guys from *Star Trek: Voyager* was in it. Gina claimed that it was a classic, but her opinion hardly counts in such situations. Besides, Wayne and I had the votes.

Gina's stacking glasses into a dish rack.

'I forgot to tell you. I finished Issue 9,' she says.

'Excellent,' I enthuse. 'Got any copies on you?'

'I'll grab one for you in a minute.' She serves a couple of the regulars lurking in the dark part of the front bar.

The guy onstage in the next room speaks into the microphone, asking for more guitar in the foldback. I recognise his voice. It's Gus. Behind me, someone is playing the *Star Wars* pinball game. Jar Jar Binks is telling them they have to get the ball up the ramp for bonus points.

'Here you go.' Gina reaches under the bar and hands me a photocopied booklet with cover type that looks like it's been written with a liquid-paper pen, mainly because it has. It's the latest copy of *Zines, She Wrote*. I flip through, stopping on one page to admire my own handiwork. Four Kid Shiva strips. Very nice.

'These look good.'

'Yeah. Ever considered doing your own comics?'

'What do you think these are?'

'I mean your own *book* of comics, dickhead.'

'Oh. No, I haven't really thought about it.' My own comic? Now that's an interesting idea. But would people buy it? At the moment I'm drawing these dicky little comic strips about baby Hindu gods, and giving a couple to Gina to print in her zine. People pick up Gina's zine because it's good and because it's funny, and if they like my strips then that's a bonus. But would people actually pay specifically to see these strips? I'm not so sure. Gina likes them because she's my friend. Total strangers are another story entirely. 'I wouldn't really know where to start.'

'Print, photocopy, fold, staple. Nothing particularly complicated.'

'But you've been doing it for ages.'

'It's not brain surgery, Steven. Anyway, it could be good. You should think about it.'

'Uh-huh.' And then I'd have a box of unsold comics stashed somewhere in my room reminding me of how unfunny I can be. Maybe I'll pass, thanks. I sip my beer and flick to the CD section to read Gina's review of the first Pixies album.

'Have you thought any more about reviewing in the street press, maybe, for Van?' I ask.

'Do you think she'd be interested?'

'She suggested it—and she's the editor. Streetmags don't pay for reviews, but you could scam free copies of new releases. She said there might be some interviewing, too.'

Gina tilts her head and smiles. 'Yeah, maybe. Oops. Gotta go.' She skips off to serve the people milling about the back bar, now that there's some action happening on stage.

I fold the zine and stuff it in my pocket, then join Wayne as Gus begins his set with 'I Take it All Back'. I swig my beer and lose myself in the opening verse.

Later in the set, Trudy, one of the other bartenders, joins Gus for five songs. Standing nervously beside and slightly behind him she buries her face in the microphone and looks everywhere but into the crowd. She really has no right to be that nervous. People with talent often can't see how special they are—they know too much about how it's done. Trudy's voice trickles between the notes of Gus's guitar. He's grinning and staring at her in obvious admiration, but she doesn't notice. She focuses on the ceiling and continues to sing. Between songs she looks at Gus and he reassures her with smiles and nods. After her last song she steps down shyly from the stage and blends into the crowd.

'Damn, she's good,' says Wayne. 'Didn't you guys have something going there for a while?'

I shrug. 'A while back, yeah. We slept together a few times . . .'

'Until you found something wrong with her and dumped her.'

'Implying what, exactly?'

'Just making an observation.'

'And that would be?'

'Well . . .' He takes another mouthful of beer. 'I'm just saying that you hook up with these pretty special women and then a week or two in you don't seem to want to have much to do with them any more.'

I can't really argue with this, but I try to put my case forward. 'I just haven't met the right person yet, you know? It can take a while to find the right one. Trudy and I—we just didn't click. She didn't get my jokes and I got sick of listening to the tapes she had in the car.'

'Well, when you put it like that, it makes perfect sense.'

'Fuck you. Anyway, you can hardly talk, all the women you see.'

'But we're not talking about me. Anyway, I think you *have* met the right person. You just don't know it yet.'

I know where he's going with this one, but he's wrong. Everyone I know eventually gets around to asking what's going on between me and Gina, like we're going to turn into some kind of *When Harry Met Sally* fairytale love story or something. But they're wrong. Sure, when I first met Gina I might have had a bit of a crush on her—who wouldn't fancy someone so smart and funny and spunky? But I've never been good at making the first move. Every time something has happened between me and a girl, the girl has started it. I don't know why, but that's the way it goes. And Gina never made the move. I wasn't sure how to, or even if I really wanted to, and before I knew it she was seeing some guy from HR called Ryan and the moment had passed. So we became friends instead. And I think that's great. Better, in fact. If we had've done anything *relationshippy* together I probably would've freaked out like I always do when I start to feel—I dunno, *committed* or something. Like I have to pretend that everything's perfect between us, we're star-crossed soul-mates and every little thing they do is magic, when really I only like maybe sixty per cent of them and the rest is either just okay or else it shits me to tears—their taste in music, the smell of their breath, their pet name for me, the way they answer the phone; the fact that they snore, the gap in their teeth—and it gets so I can't remember what I liked about them in the first place. There's too much information and I can't sort the bad from the good any more so I just give up and walk away because it's easier than trying to explain myself. I know how it'll sound, and in the end 'I don't think this is working out' is pretty close to the truth anyway, and that's what's important, right? The truth. I don't have to go through any of that with Gina because we're just mates. Relationships may come and go, but mates are for ever. Try getting the outside world to understand that a guy and a girl *can* be just mates, though. Sometimes I think that's even harder than the whole relationship bullshit thing.

'I don't want to have this discussion again, Wayne.'

'Fair enough. I'm just saying, is all.'

The second band is setting up, assembling their drum kit and plugging guitars into amps. I sip my beer in silence. This'll be my last one. I've got to start early tomorrow, so that I'll have time to get used to Aki's run. I should be thinking of it as my run now, but I'll live in that strange, hopeful land of denial for a little longer. I'll allow myself to believe that tomorrow I'll find Dave has been replaced by an identical robot duplicate, programmed with a sense of fairness and compassion. I'll get to work, park my bike, and Robot Dave will walk up to me, his metallic steps ringing quietly on the concrete floor, and he'll tell me I can have my run back, and I can have a raise as well. I'll smile into his electronic eyes and say, 'Thanks, Dave. I knew you'd come through with the goods', and he'll wink an inhuman wink and say, 'No problem, Steven', before clanking off to Best Street, where he'll use the lasers hidden in his index fingers to set fire to that crazy old Scottish bitch in retaliation for daring to imply that employees of Australia Post are anything other than honest and good.

I finish my beer and smack the glass down on the table. 'I'm off,' I tell Wayne.

'Split a taxi?'

'You going my way?'

'Ah, yeah. I thought I'd drop in on Anthea—your place is close.'

'How're those communication problems?'

'Well, I thought I'd see what I could do about them tonight.'

'Wayne, you're the consummate romantic. Three beers drunk and stinking of pub smoke, you're going to win back the heart of your ladylove, hey?'

He punches me on the shoulder and rests his other arm around me. 'Nothing solves communication problems like beer.'

We wave to Gina at the bar. 'Going home,' I call out.

She mouths, 'Wait a sec.'

Wayne heads out the door to find a cab.

'I've had a think,' Gina says.

'Yeah?'

'I think we can clear your name.'

'Yeah?' Here it comes. The Idea. This should be interesting.

'Yeah. Look, we know that you didn't kill Satan, right?'

I nod.

'Which means that someone or something else is responsible for his death, right?'

'Yeah . . .'

'Well, I got thinking. What would Jessica Fletcher do in this situation?'

'You want me to pick out a really nice grey knitted turtleneck and book an appointment for a perm?'

'Ha, ha. She'd investigate, wouldn't she? And the first thing to do in order to find out who killed Satan is to determine cause of death, right?'

'Right . . .'

'So, we find out which vet the Scottish woman took the dog to.'

'Okay . . .'

'And get them to do an autopsy.'

And there it is. The Idea. Cut the dog up to see what killed it and go from there. I'm gob-smacked. It's a slightly more serious undertaking than gluing up a bunch of posters on High Street. I try to work out if I should have expected such a suggestion from Gina, but this is pretty out there even for her.

'Look, I've got to keep working, but I'll do a ring-around tomorrow to find the vet. You give me a call and I'll fill you in.'

I try to express my reservations in the most diplomatic way possible. I'm thinking fraud, police, dog guts, but I simply say, 'I don't know, Gina, that sounds a little . . .'

'A little what?'

'Radical.'

She fixes me with a look that expertly combines exasperation with you're-just-chicken. She's stopped listening. 'Steven. I've thought this through. It'll work.'

I try again. 'You don't think it might be just a bit too . . . imaginative?'

'Trust me.'

She is definitely not listening. 'Okay, whatever,' I shrug. If there's one thing I've learned with Gina, it's that once she has an Idea, the worst thing you can do is tell her why she can't or shouldn't act on it. So when she says things like, 'We should gatecrash Satan's autopsy', the best thing I can do is let her say it. It's not like I could stop her, anyway. Maybe I can minimise the damage somehow, by joining in. And maybe it'll all turn out okay and kind of fun, despite the fraud, police and dog guts. It's hard to tell with Gina.

'I'll call you after work,' I say, thinking that by tomorrow she might be distracted by a fresh Idea. If she isn't, I'll have to give the reasonable approach another try.

'What took you so long, man?'

'Gina's going to clear my name.'

'Yeah?'

'It's a case of WWJD.'

'WWJD?'

'What Would Jessica Do?'

Wayne laughs.

I let the taxi carry us home. Thinking about the look of determination on Gina's face, I feel more than a little out of my depth.

THURSDAY

At three-thirty I arrive home, banging the front door open. I shrug out of my reflector vest and fling it onto the couch.

'Missed me,' Van says, not looking up from painting her toenails.

I grunt and make my way to the bathroom, undoing my shirt as I go. I slide the door closed and tear off my clothes. I hook a finger into my socks and yank them off as I turn the hot tap on full. I lather my body and hold my head so that all I can hear is the roar of water in each ear. I concentrate on the physicality of the shower, its temperature, the water on my shoulders, the water running around my feet, and I let out a sigh that I've been holding in all day. My muscles loosen and the skin on my arms begins to warm. Aki's run is a bastard. My legs tremble in exhaustion as I stand, eyes closed, slowly running my soapy hands over my body. Calm down, I tell myself. It's only the first day. It'll take a while to get used to it. In the meantime, though, I think I'll just hate it. I miss my cats. It's like starting from scratch again. It's all unfamiliar and it's much more like work than I want it to be. Rucker's Hill on an old one-gear back-braked travesty of an Australia Post bicycle is a bitch, pure and simple. I let out another sigh and turn the taps off. I dry myself and climb back into my shorts and shirt, then go and flick on the TV. It's that weird Italian cartoon with the two plasticine monsters. I sit on the armchair and watch them babble to each other as a plasticine butterfly alights on one head, then the other. They try to swat it, but it stays just out of reach.

'How was work?' asks Van, dipping her brush back into the bottle.

I keep staring at the TV. 'Don't ask.'

'Not good, then.'

The two monsters now have a butterfly net and are chasing the butterfly on and off the screen.

Van draws the brush over her smallest toenail, coating it with a vivid purple. I stare at her feet, and realise that from this angle I can see along the curve of her thigh and underneath the loose skirt that she's wearing. I catch myself staring, then blush and turn back to the TV. One of the monsters has the butterfly net embedded in its head.

I stand up in order to remove the temptation of checking out Van's legs again, and head for my room. Not that I think Van would really mind if I did—she's pretty open about sex and all that stuff. Once I walked in on her and Sean shagging on the lounge-room couch, and I was the most embarrassed of the three of us. Van didn't even cover herself up. She just lay there on Sean's chest and made small-talk with me until I backed off into my room and tried not to listen through the wall. Van tried to make a joke out of it later, but I was still too embarrassed to laugh along. There's something fundamentally unnerving about seeing your housemate naked. It changes the nature of your relationship in a subtle but freaky way. These days I listen carefully for any suspiciously rhythmic sounds before I come out of my room.

My calves still feel sore, but the shower has relaxed me a little. Now that I'm less grumpy, it's time to get on with the day's proceedings. I need to enact a little damage control vis-a-vis Gina and the dog autopsy. Hopefully, she won't have done anything yet, and I'll be able to talk her out of it somehow.

As I dial I try to imagine the kind of bullshit she would spin in order to get the information she wants. I have no doubt she'll get it if she tries. Whether she's looking for an original pressing of a Radiohead EP or an interview subject for her zine, she pretty much always comes up with the goods. I have to admit that I am curious about Satan, but something tells me it's better to let sleeping dogs lie than tell a lie in order to wake up a dead dog.

'Hi, you've called Gina and Carla. We're all out stealing cars right now, but if you leave a message after the lady says to leave a message, with a brief description of what model and make you're after, we'll get back to you.' There's a silence and then the robot Telstra lady tells me to leave a message and then to press hash or hang up. I've never understood the point of the first option. I mean, you press hash and it ends the message, sure, but that just leaves you standing there with the phone in your hand. If you want to make another call you have to hang up anyway, so what's the point of the hash-then-hang-up sequence? The illusion of choice, I suppose.

I leave my message and hang up, ignoring the hash option.

I sit down at my computer and open up the Kid Shiva strips I've been working on, but I'm too frazzled by the long day to do anything creative. I check my email instead, hoping for some kind of amusing distraction. No such luck. All that comes up in the inbox is a string of crap from various newsletters I subscribe to, and a couple of spams about D-cup schoolgirls. Nothing that could be considered the electronic equivalent of a handwritten envelope. Realising that the lack of emails *from* actual human beings is probably a result of the lack of emails *to* actual humans, I click on a random name in my address book and fire off a letter to Joe, a guy from London I met on a bulletin board dedicated to the work of an obscure Scottish conspiracy-theorist comic writer. I'm halfway through telling Joe about the latest debacle in my work life when the phone rings.

'Hey.' It's Gina. 'How was work?'

'Sucky.'

'Poor boy. Well, I've got some good news for you. He's at the North Fitzroy Veterinary Clinic.'

'You mean Satan? That was quick.'

'What can I say? I got the power.'

'So what now?' I'm just going with the flow at this point, trying to work out the best time to mention that lying to get someone else's dog autopsied might be considered a criminal activity. I'm sure an opportunity will present itself soon.

'Now we go round and visit.'

'We do?'

'Sure. I told the vet I was the old lady's niece, and that she was too distraught to call personally. They weren't sure to begin with, but I sweet-talked them.'

'I bet you did.'

'So you wanna go check it out?'

This line of investigation is likely to get us into trouble in the long run, but it seems a shame to waste the effort that Gina has gone to. I try to be as open to new experiences as I possibly can, and this is definitely a new experience. Icky, but undeniably new. 'When were you thinking?'

'How about now?'

'Now?'

'It's a dead dog, Steven. It's not going to keep for very long, is it?'

'I guess not.'

'Okay, cool. I'll come round now and pick you up.'

I try out various 'let's be reasonable' speeches, while I ponder what would be the best thing to wear to the viewing of a dog's corpse. Green shoes? No, I think Docs are probably more appropriate autopsy-wear. Maybe I'm being too sensitive—this could answer a few questions for me. I've seen dead dogs before. Hell, I've seen *this* dead dog before. I decide on the brown corduroy shirt and black suit coat. Shabby formal.

Gina is all in black—black skirt, black stockings, black jumper. Her hair's a little redder than usual. She's tied it back, but a few loose strands have worked loose and drift in front of her face. Shabby formal.

'You dye your hair?'

'I did it Sunday night. Wondered how long before you'd notice.'

'It was dark in the pub.'

'Good excuse. Hi, Van.'

Van waves. 'How you doing, spunky?'

'Not bad.'

'Steven mentioned something about you wanting to write for us?'

Gina frowns slightly. I try to look innocent. It doesn't work. I stop.

'Because if you are interested,' says Van, 'then so are we.'

I don't often see Gina embarrassed. It's oddly refreshing.

'Well, I don't know—I've never really reviewed anything official before.' She scratches her left arm shyly.

'It's not that hard. You just write what you think. I like what you've done in your zine.'

'Really?' She stops scratching.

'Yeah. Why don't you give me a call at work tomorrow so we can talk a bit more about it?'

'That'd be great, Van. Thanks.' Gina giggles.

I lean against the doorframe trying not to look smug, but it's hard not to be smug when you've successfully micro-managed a good friend's life in a beneficial direction.

We pull up outside the chicken wholesalers a few doors down from the vet.

'Let me do the talking,' Gina says firmly.

'Sure thing, Jess. But there is one thing I should point out.'

'What?'

'Even if we do find out who killed Satan, we're going to be left with a nagging suspicion that you're the real murderer.'

'What?'

'You know—every week Jessica finds a dead body somewhere and "solves" the crime. But Jessica's presence is the common factor in every murder. The circumstantial evidence is pretty damning.'

'You're an idiot.'

'I'm not the one about to enter a vet's surgery to look at a dead dog.'

'Yes, you are.'

She skips up onto the footpath and into the vet's. That was the perfect opportunity to voice my objections, and I missed it.

It's a quiet day for sick animals. The only other person in the clinic is a man with an empty goldfish bowl resting on his lap. He's dressed in brown corduroy pants and a navy tracksuit-top, the kind that zips up the front. His stringy hair is plastered to the top of his head like the beginnings of a comb-over. A little plastic castle inside the fish bowl looks forlorn without anything swimming around it.

'Can I help you?' The receptionist is wearing a long white coat and holding a wad of cotton in the palm of her hand, on which sits a bagel-sized terrapin. It has a thin white strip wound around one leg. 'Mr Peters?' She proffers the terrapin to the man with the bowl.

'Is he all right?'

The receptionist smiles. 'He'll be just fine. Only two stitches. The tricky part was waterproofing the bandages, but they should hold long enough.'

Mr Peters rests his fish bowl on the desk and picks up the turtle by the shell. He brings it level with his face. 'Did the nasty pusscat give Eric a scare?' he burbles. Eric responds by tucking his neck back into his shell and flailing his legs in the air as though he's swimming. Mr Peters plops Eric into the bowl. Eric promptly pokes his head out again and does a slow lap, before settling on top of the plastic castle, his neck stretched, his nose above the water level.

'Are you sure that bowl's big enough for him?' Gina asks.

'This is just Eric's travelling bowl. He's got a three-metre tank back at home.' Mr Peters picks up the bowl and slowly walks out the door without spilling a drop of water. I guess he's an expert at transporting terrapins. The bell jingles behind him.

'Now. What can I do for you two?' asks the receptionist.

Gina beams her best smile. 'Hi. I called earlier today. Mrs Fraser's niece. I rang about her dog.'

'Oh, yes, I remember. You wanted to see Gavin before he was cremated?'

'Gavin?'

'The dog,' says the receptionist.

Oops. I forgot to tell Gina about Satan's secret identity. Not five minutes into the plan and we've fucked it already. Ah, well. Maybe it's for the best. Now we can get on with something less risky, like tracking down the Heavy Product guy.

Gavin. What a stupid name. What is it with people who give dogs human names, anyway? Some work fine, like Lizzie, Dave or Bob, but names like Gavin just sound dumb. I once knew a dog called Anthony, but Gavin has got to be the most un-doglike name I've ever heard.

'Oh, right, I keep forgetting. That's his full name. We always called him by his nickname. Jeeves. Haven't heard him called "Gavin" for ages.' Gina laughs a laugh that's supposed to sound dismissive, but I can hear the nerves. I'll be impressed if the receptionist buys it.

'How do you get "Jeeves" from "Gavin"?' she asks.

'Well, when I was little and learning to spell, I kept going around chanting "D-O-G" whenever I saw Gavin, and then it escalated into "D-O-G, G for Gavin" as a little chant, and then I took to calling him "G-for-Gavin" and that got shortened to "G-for"—you know, like some people call their dogs "Deefa"?'

'I've always hated that name,' I chime in, for the sake of verisimilitude. The receptionist flicks me a who-asked-you kind of look before Gina goes on.

'Well,' Gina says, 'we shortened it to simply "G". And it stuck like that. It's not as though you could shorten it any further.'

'Unless you called the dog "guh",' says the receptionist, enunciating the phoneme. I giggle. G for giggle.

'Yes, well,' says Gina, sounding slightly breathless by this stage, 'except when my little brother was born, he used to mispronounce "G", and started calling him Jeeves instead. And we all just followed his example.'

The receptionist is staring at Gina as if she's an idiot, but it seems she's bought the story. 'Well, Gavin's through here, if you'd like to see him.'

'That would be nice. I'd like to say goodbye to him. And there's something I'd like to ask, as well.'

We follow the receptionist out the back, into a cavernous room with a leather-upholstered table in the middle. Between two benches on the right-hand wall is a large metal door.

'He's in the freezer,' says the receptionist, motioning to the metal door.

She puts on a lined parka and opens up the freezer door, pushing down hard on the handle.

'Did you manage to determine the cause of death?' asks Gina.

'Well, we had assumed that it was something he ate.'

'You haven't done the autopsy yet, then?'

The receptionist stares at her. 'The what?'

'The autopsy.'

She frowns at Gina. It's partially a frown of confusion, but there's some indignant something-or-other in there as well. 'You want a necropsy?' she asks. 'I'm sorry, Miss . . .'

'Reynolds.'

'Miss Reynolds. I'm afraid that only your aunt herself can request a necropsy. It's a rather delicate and serious matter, best left to the next of kin.'

'But I am next of kin,' Gina says.

'Well, technically, yes,' says the receptionist, 'but you weren't Gavin's actual owner, if you see what I mean.'

'But my aunt asked me to enquire about the possibility. She just wanted to be sure—you know, to be sure that she was right about her suspicions.'

'Her suspicions?'

Gina clears her throat. 'She thinks—though I don't necessarily agree—that her mailman poisoned Gavin—Jeeves—with some chicken or something.'

'She thinks her mailman killed her dog?'

'Yes.'

'But that's *ridiculous*!' I say. 'Whoever heard of something so patently ludicrous?'

Both Gina and the receptionist stare at me. That same look again.

'Well, it is pretty dumb, don't you think?' I say, sheepishly. 'A mailman murdering a dog. Stupid. If you ask me.'

'As I was saying, Miss Reynolds,' the receptionist ignores me, 'only your aunt herself can ask me to perform a necropsy. I can understand why she would want such a thing, but there are procedures to follow.'

'Aunt Abby asked me to ask on her behalf. She doesn't want to be there for it, but she does want to know for sure if it was the mailman. She's too traumatised by the loss to come in person. I'm sure you under-stand.' With this last, Gina goes into her uber-charming mode, only just stopping short of batting her eyelashes.

'Of course it wasn't the mailman,' I say. 'That's just stupid.'

'Steven, can you be quiet, please?'

I shut up.

'Look,' says the receptionist. 'If your aunt calls me tomorrow morning, I can do the necropsy in the afternoon. Tell her that she doesn't have to be here, but that I do need to speak to her personally.'

Gina nods. 'Well, okay. I'll get Aunt Abby to call you tomorrow, but could I still just see Jeeves now?'

'Certainly. I'll bring him out.' She opens the freezer door again and steps inside.

'Why would the receptionist do the autopsy?' I whisper.

'Necropsy. She's not the receptionist. She's the vet.'

'But she was behind the desk,'

'She's wearing a white coat.'

'I can see that. I thought it was just a uniform.'

'It is. A vet's uniform.'

Our squabble is interrupted by a cry from the vet.

The two of us bound towards the freezer. The vet is standing beside a stainless-steel trolley. There is no Doberman corpse to be seen. Above the trolley, on the side wall of the freezer, which would be the back wall of the surgery, is a small window, about two metres from the floor. Directly underneath is a pile of shattered glass.

'I don't believe it,' says the vet. 'Someone's stolen your dog.'

'Oh, no you're not.'

'Why not?' Gina pulls her innocent face.

'Because lying to vets is just lying. Lying to the police is deception, or fraud or something.'

Gina takes a nonchalant sip of her coffee and looks away. I'm left with my not-all-that-convincing cautionary tone hanging in the air. I try to make her meet my gaze. She flicks her eyes around the room, pretending to read the posters, but I know she's just trying to psych me out.

'Steven, this is our first real lead. We have to follow it up.'

'Fine. Follow it up. But follow it up some other way.'

'If you have any suggestions, I'd be happy to consider them.'

I pause. Of course I don't have any suggestions. I suck the dregs of my coffee. Now it's my turn to stare at the posters.

'You have to admit you're curious,' Gina says. 'And you have to admit it's pretty suspicious. Someone steals the very dog that you've been falsely accused of murdering, before it can have an autopsy performed. Why would they do that?'

'Because they're insane?'

'Because they have something to hide. Because they were the ones responsible for Gavin's death, and they don't want to be found out. So if we find the people who stole the dog, we can find out how and maybe even why they did it. Either way, it clears your name.'

'There never was going to be an autopsy,' I insist.

'Necropsy. Yes, there was. Aunt Abby was going to arrange one.'

'I've heard your Scottish accent. It isn't very convincing.'

'You've never heard it over the phone.'

'Yes, I have. Remember that time you did the Highland Games answering machine message?'

'That wasn't me. That was Mum.'

'Really? I could've sworn it was you.'

'Well, it's academic now. We need to concentrate on the facts to hand.' She pulls a notebook and a pen out of her bag and flips to the first page. 'I bought this today. It's my casebook.'

'Promise me one thing,' I say.

'What?'

'You won't get shitty when I tell the cops I've never met you before in my life?'

She grins. 'I wouldn't expect anything less from you, Steven.'

'As long as we've got that straight.'

'Sure. Anyway, I'm not going to lie to anyone. I'm going to call Matt and ask if he can do me a favour.'

'Matt?'

'You remember him—tall, dark hair? I was kind of seeing him earlier this year.'

'The big guy? The footy-head?'

'Yeah, that's him. He's a cop.'

'You know, that doesn't surprise me at all.'

'Anyway, we've kind of stayed in touch and I thought I'd give him a call to see if he can find out anything about the report of Satan being stolen.'

'Gavin.'

'Whatever.'

'Kind of stayed in touch? What does that mean?'

'It means I saw him a couple of weeks ago at Meyers Place and he bought me a drink.'

'And?'

'And I'm calling in a favour. That's all.' She rips the lid off of the pen with her teeth, and begins writing. 'You can head off, if you want,' she says.

'Okay,' I say. 'Want to meet up at the pub tonight? You working?'

'Yeah, I'm doing close tonight.'

'I'll come by about nine, yeah?'

'Okay, see you then.' She doesn't look up from her casebook.

At the tram stop, there's a new Heavy Product sticker stuck over the timetable information. I make a mental note to mention it to Gina tonight, so she can add it to the list. The tram sidles up and I plonk myself on the steps right at the back. No ticket inspector on this section, so I slink ticket-less from the tram and walk the short stretch back home, practising my lines for when Gina gets busted for impersonating a bereaved dog-owner.

'Me? I've never met this woman before in my life! She said what? No, she's definitely making that up, officer.'

'Making what up?' asks Van.

'Nothing—just babbling to myself,' I say, ducking into my bedroom.

I boot up my computer and look at my desk. Things are getting a little cluttered around here. The papers that have been arranged into the important pile have slid out from under each other, creating an important puddle. I flick the corners of the topmost few: a doctor's bill, a super-annuation statement and an invitation to a dance party that I didn't go to last week. I'm hanging on to the invitation because it has a really cool cartoon of a monkey in a tuxedo on it. I wish I could draw like that. I especially wish I could draw monkeys like that but, sadly, my drawing abilities are stunted. To compensate, I work within my limitations. Utilising basic geometric shapes and brightly coloured patterns to make up the main characters of the Kid Shiva strip allows me to harness the iconic representation that is such an important part of children's drawing. At least that's what I tell people when they ask. Plus, they look cute with their big round bubbly heads.

I open up an unfinished strip. I've got Hanuman and Shiva discussing the famous physics thought-experiment put forward in the thirties by a guy called Schrödinger to prove how absurd some of the claims of the new science of quantum physics were. I've never been a hundred per cent sure of this experiment and exactly what it means, but the last time I read *In Search of Schrödinger's Cat* I reckon I came close to actually getting it. Even if I don't understand Schrödinger's cat, I've always liked the weirdness of the concept. I'm pretty sure Hanuman's explanation is inaccurate, but what the hell—it's a comic strip, not a textbook. I can always blame any inaccuracy on Hanuman's lack of comprehension instead of mine.

I muck around for a while, re-sizing pictures and shortening dialogue. I think about what I'm going to do with these guys once they're finished. I Maybe Gina's right—maybe I should be thinking bigger. Maybe I'm ready to put my own comic together. How many strips would I need for that? Ten? Twenty? I've done about twenty so far—would that be enough? And of course, there's the other question: does the world really need a series of poorly drawn gag strips featuring bastardised Indian gods rehashing old vaudeville routines and regurgitating popular science? I suppose there's only one way to find out.

Okay, yeah. Let's do this. Let's make a comic. I open up the twenty best, and while I'm waiting for them to print out I dial up the Internet and go for a surf. I find out about a new series of *Blue Monday*, on comicsactuallyworthreading.com. I check out my favourite blog to see if Hot Soup Girl has put up a new entry, but she hasn't. I log in to her guestbook under an assumed name and bawl her out for slacknesss before heading over to a music industry gossip page where I discover that the forthcoming Ray Fayne album is either going to be called 'Binary Love' or 'Going Head-to-Head with the Powers-That-Used-to-Be'. I take a detour to his official site, which is asking viewers to cast a vote as to which of the two titles they prefer.

Finally, I check my email. It's all crap. Probably should have sent that email to Joe. I pull it out of the drafts folder, but I can't really be arsed sitting in front of this screen any longer and I save it back as a draft. I look at my watch. Five-thirty now, a few hours before I have to head over to the Empress. Enough time to let these strips print out and then cobble together some dinner to eat in front of prime-time TV. After the day I've had, I could seriously use a nice long dose of meaningless crap. I head to the lounge, leaving the printer clunking and buzzing behind me.

It's well past ten by the time I cycle down to the Empress. Gina is standing by herself behind the bar. I pull up a stool and frown at the sound of the ambitious guitar band coming from the lounge.

'Who's playing?'

Gina hands me a beer. 'Didn't catch their name,' she says. 'They're the support. Not particularly impressive, whoever they are. This kind of middle-of-the-road indie pop-rock with a heavy backbeat and nerd-nasal vocals doesn't really do it for me.'

'You what?'

'Hey, if I'm going to be a music reviewer, I need to talk like one.'

'I'd say you've got it going on there.'

'You try.'

'Okay, how's this? "A neo-baroque rendering of traditional four-piece garage-rock stylings, melding perfectly with contemporary sensibilities and issues-based lyrics".'

'Not bad. How about "post-punk-pop for the new millennium, angry, exhibitionist and relentlessly danceable"?'

'Pseudo-classical riffwork laced with drum-and-bass flavours and addictively cute vocals.'

'Aggressively bastardising skacore and skiffle with an overlay of dependable rhythm torn from the bosom of Sugar Hill.'

'New new romantic for the new generation, blending saccharine keyboard melodies with robotic drum sequences.'

We both break up laughing.

Two crusty-looking guys come up to the bar. One of them is short and stocky, with a matted blond beard, and the other is tall and skinny with rainbow-coloured dreadlocks.

'Hey, Gina, how are you tonight?' asks Matted-beard.

'Yeah, well, you know. I'm at work. What can I get you?'

'Two Mountain Goats, please.'

Gina fills two glasses with the cloudy fluid. While they wait the two guys sway back and forth on their feet in the classic autistic style of the bong-smoker. Gina hands the glasses to Matted-beard. He heads through to the band area. Rainbow-dreads follows, hands inside his pants as he frantically scratches his arse.

'Classy clientele you've got in this establishment,' I say, motioning to the hippies.

'Yeah, they come out in droves when Zircon Encrusted Tweezers play. Those guys are like their roadies or something. They carried the drums in earlier.'

'Can't imagine the Tweezers' neuvo-prog would follow this indie shite particularly well.'

'Shan tries to put a bit of diversity in the line-up. Sometimes it works.'

'So how'd things with Matt go?' I ask.

'He didn't know anything. But he said he'd keep his ears open. What you been up to?'

'Oh, not much. Some comic strip stuff. I wanted to ask you about how to put a comic together. I mean, I've got the comics, but I'm not sure how to make it into a book thing.'

'No problem. You're gonna make a Kid Shiva comic?'

'Yeah, I got thinking about what you said and I figured, why not?'

'That's really good, Steven. I think it'll be great. Hang on a sec.'

She serves a couple wearing Jane's Addiction T-shirts. I sit back and listen to the indie nerd-rockers in the next room. They finish playing, and the bar gets busy for a while, so I just watch Gina handling all the wankers, the indie-kids, the hippies and the crusties who make hanging out at the Empress their own personalised badge of coolness.

Later that night, after close, Gina and I are on the same side of the bar, a bottle of gin with the free-pour lid still attached sitting between us. The pinball machine is silent and the lights are all off, except for the front bar.

'Thought they'd never leave,' says Gina.

'You chased them out, though.'

'You get good at it after a while. Even if you have to just stand there behind them screaming, "FUCK OFF HOME! FUCK OFF HOME!" well, if that's what it takes then that's what it takes.'

'You've got a flair for that kind of thing.'

'So anyway, I've been thinking. It's time to kick this investigation into second gear.'

Investigation? That sounds perilously official. 'Yeah?'

'Yup. I think it's time we had a stake-out.'

'A what?'

'A stake-out. We've got to stake out the back of the vet's surgery to see if whoever stole Satan comes back. The surgery backs onto Best Street, so we can keep an eye on the old lady's house as well.'

'How opportune.'

'I know. So, what we need to do is take my car and park it just outside the bottle shop. Look, I'll show you.'

She gets out her casebook and shows me a hand-drawn map of the corner of Scotchmer and Best Streets, with the vet's, the bottle shop and the supermarket all drawn in. She's even drawn a little picture of a car next to the bottle shop with the word 'us' circled above it.

'You have been busy, haven't you?'

'Like I said, we don't have much time. I'm not working until late tomorrow, so if we get there about six, we'll have a few hours to check everything out.'

I recognise the familiar sensation of being bundled along, and nod. 'Just like Emilio Estevez and Richard Dreyfuss, hey?'

'Except I hope neither of us ends up sleeping with Mrs Fraser. Or the vet.'

'She was kind of cute.'

'Mrs Fraser?'

'Yeah, Mrs Fraser. The four-foot-tall Scottish banshee whose dog tried to kill me every morning for the last six months. I think she's cute.'

'Banshees are Irish.'

'You know what I mean.'

Gina closes her book and packs it away. 'How's the new run?'

'Sucks,' I say, finishing off my gin.

'Don't worry, we'll get your old one back.'

'You know, Gina, I don't know if it actually works that way.'

'No harm trying, is there? Anyway, I'd better lock up now.'

I shrug and open the door. Outside, the wind has picked up. A solitary guy with a canvas satchel strapped to his back and a skateboard tucked under his arm walks past. He pats the side of the pub with one hand and strolls on. I notice that he's left something behind where he touched the wall. Gina comes out and locks the door behind her.

'Oh, shit,' I say, nudging Gina.

She looks to where I'm pointing. Just underneath the blackboard announcing next week's gigs is a Heavy Product sticker.

'That wasn't there before, was it?'

'What?'

'The sticker, for fuck's sake.'

'Oh. No. No, it wasn't.'

'It's him, then. We've found him!' I shout, and take off after the boy with the skateboard. 'Come on!'

Something must've given me away, because just as I'm about to throw my hand onto the guy's shoulder to tell him how much I admire his work, he glances back and sees that I'm closing in. He kicks into a loping sprint, outpacing me easily to the next roundabout, then drops his board and with two simple kicks, he glides away. I stop and bend double, heaving wheezy breaths, and am vaguely comforted by the arrival, some thirty seconds later, of Gina, huffing mightily.

'These fell out of his backpack,' she says between breaths, handing me a wad of stickers all bearing the Heavy Product logo.

'Did you recognise him?' I puff.

'No, did you?'

'No.' I straighten slightly, staring at the stickers as if they might give me some clue. Of course they don't. I concentrate on breathing normally and arrange the stickers into a neat stack.

'We missed him.'

'Next time.'

Slowly, I hand Gina half the stickers.

FRIDAY

My feet are sunk beneath a pile of chip packets, empty envelopes and pages that have fallen out of Gina's *Melways*. She sits behind the wheel, staring intently across the street. I'm looking over her shoulder, squinting out the window.

'I can't see anything happening.'

'sssSSSSSHHhhhh!'

The street is quiet and empty. It's twenty past six. The sky is a washed-out pink, starting to get dark. My feet rustle under the rubbish. Gina shifts in her seat, adjusts it, pushes it back for more leg room, and sighs. I click on the radio.

'. . . *more of your favourite hits over the next two hours, thanks to the people at*—'

Gina clicks it off and glares at me.

'Well, what am I supposed to be doing? This is boring.'

'It's not supposed to be exciting.'

I lean back and cross my ankles, letting out a melodramatic sigh. 'Well, good. Because it isn't.'

Gina ignores me and picks up the casebook. She jots something down.

'What are you writing?'

'Notes.'

I grunt and count the different chip flavours represented on the floor of her car. I glance at the clock. It's twenty-three minutes past six. I click the radio back on.

'. . . *in the next hour we'll be celebrating another of our commercial-free forties, with forty minutes of uninterrupted—*'

'Steven!'

I sigh loudly for emphasis. 'It's Friday night, Gina.'

'Sshhh! Someone's coming!'

A man carrying a pair of plastic grocery bags is walking along the footpath. He pauses for a moment to tie up his shoelaces. As he passes Number 58, Gina holds her breath. We watch him walk the length of the block and turn left into Park Street. Gina writes the man into her surveillance record. I wish I'd brought something to read.

The streetlights flicker on. A couple of cats wander past. I walk to the bottle shop and buy two Coopers stubbies. We sit and nuzzle them in silence as North Fitzroy begins its Friday night routine, which, for the back of the vet surgery and Mrs Fraser, seems to involve not very much at all.

'We don't even know she's in there.'

'It doesn't matter. If she is, she'll come out some time. If she's not, she'll come home some time.'

'Some time? How long are we going to hang around?'

'Don't panic. I'm working tonight, so you can go home after that.'

This is stupid. I thought Gina was trying to be Jessica Fletcher, but this is more like one of those black-and-white detective films with Humphrey Bogart. Long and boring.

'Well, if we're here for the night, then I'm going to get more beer.'

By nine o'clock, six empty stubbies lie on the floor, their labels picked off and scattered amongst the other litter. I've angled my seat back as far as it will go and I'm lying with my eyes closed, feeling the beer slosh around my stomach and thinking we should've eaten beforehand.

'Hey,' Gina nudges me.

'What?' I open my eyes.

'There.' She points to two guys leaving the front yard of the house next door to Number 56. They pause for a moment at their gate and then move off along the street, turning right into Scotchmer. They walk slowly, casually. It's Rainbow-dreads and Matted-beard.

'They live around here?'

'Hm,' says Gina, scribbling in her notebook.

I notice that the veranda light at Number 56 is off. 'So she was home.'

'Yeah, I think she must have gone to bed—it turned off about ten minutes ago.'

'So we can go, then?'

'Okay, yes. We can go. I don't think we'll see anything else tonight.' Gina turns the ignition key and passes me her notebook. 'Hold this?'

I open Gina's casebook and flick on the overhead light. We head down to Brunswick Street. Gina has made a note for every half-hour we were parked. Occasionally there's a note between the half-hours.

'So who's your lead suspect, then? The grocery bag guy? The three giggling girls? Or one of the cats?'

'It's too early to tell right now,' Gina says without taking her eyes off the road.

'My money's on the cats. Makes sense, really. Cats and dogs are natural enemies. In cartoons, at least.'

'So are posties and dogs.'

I ignore that. 'Where we heading?'

'I thought we should debrief quickly before I start work. Coffee at Deb's?'

'Ooh, Deb's. Orange poppyseed cake.'

'Exactly. I figured if you were stuffing cake down your throat I wouldn't have to listen to you whinging.'

'I wasn't whinging,'

'"Why can't I listen to the radio? When can we go? I'm *boooooored*",' Gina puts on a high-pitched child's voice. 'No, not whinging at all.'

'Well, it wasn't the most exciting Friday night I've ever had.'

'I'm sorry, Steven. I didn't realise that proving your innocence and helping you get your run back wasn't enough incentive. I didn't realise I had to entertain you as well.'

I point out a parallel parking space on our left, but Gina shakes her head. She's looking for something less challenging. Gina is crap at parallel parking. I don't mention this, however, because she always comes back at me with a comment about how I don't drive, to which I say that if I did drive I'd make sure I was able to pull off a decent parallel park before I put myself on the road. The mood she's in right now, the borderline friendly jibes of that routine could easily cross over into genuine antagonism. We park in a back street and walk.

Inside Deb's, the Friday night crowd is starting to build. We take a table in the back room. Sally drops menus on us and hustles back to the throng.

'I think tonight went well,' Gina says.

I nod non-committally and look over my shoulder at the cakes on display.

Gina taps her menu on the edge of the table. 'So do you have any ideas who might have done it?'

'Huh?'

'The dog, dummy.'

'Oh. No, not really. I'm not sure. I mean, who'd want to murder a dog? I don't know anyone like that.'

'Well, have you seen anyone suspicious lurking around?'

'"Lurking around"? How do you know if someone's lurking or not?'

'I don't know, do I? Just . . . I don't know, has anything weird happened on your run lately?'

'You mean aside from being accused of the murder of a dog by an ancient Scottish banshee?'

'Banshees are Irish.' Gina frowns at me. It's a good frown.

I think for a moment. Suspicious things on my run. Wayne turning up late for work? Not suspicious. Dave being nice to me? That would be suspicious, but it'd never happen. And then I remember Mr R. Thompson, the wacky-pants goatee dude from last week.

'Yeah, actually—there was this one guy who said something weird to me about black dogs pouncing.'

'Really?' Gina grabs her notebook. 'Black dogs pouncing? That could be significant. When was this?'

I think back. 'The day Satan turned up dead . . . Wait a minute—you don't think he—'

'It's worth checking out. What was his address?'

'Rae Street. Number thirty-something.'

'This could be our first lead.'

'I should point out that he also called me "Natasha". I don't think he was of sound mind, really.'

'Seems to me he fits the classic profile of the dog-killer.'

'You just made that up.'

'Here's Sally.'

Sally saunters over and we order coffees, which go some way to waking me up after the three-hour beer-and-snooze session I've just been through.

Gina downs her latte and looks at her watch. 'Shit. I'm going to be late. You right to get home?'

'Yeah, I'm just meeting Wayne across the road later anyway.'

'What's on?'

'He's reading at Bar Open tonight.'

'Sounds riveting.'

'Yeah, it'll be fun. You should come sometime.'

'No thank you. Wayne's painful enough without the aid of a micro-phone.'

'He's an acquired taste, that's all.'

'A taste I have no desire to acquire, thanks all the same.'

'Fair enough.'

'I'll call you about Rae Street tomorrow, okay?'

'Sure,' I say. Excellent. Nothing like the future promise of sitting in a filthy car in the dark for a whole evening to get you in the mood for beer. I head over to the reading.

'So, whaddaya think?' says Wayne.

Onstage, a tall skinny guy dressed in black jeans and a purple jumper is reading a poem about being on a train and watching men in suits. He doesn't seem to like men in suits.

People are clustered around tables or slouching on couches up against the far wall, downing their drinks and talking quietly. The guy onstage pauses for a moment. There's a polite smattering of applause.

'Thanks. Some of you might've heard this next one.' He grins and takes the microphone out, setting the stand to one side. 'It's about someone who's dear to my heart and yours, Mr Don Burke.'

There's a whoop of approval from the audience.

Wayne nudges me. 'This one's really good.'

The guy pauses for dramatic effect and then takes a deep breath. 'DOOOOOOOOONNNNNNNNN BUUUUUURRRRRRRRKKKKKKKKK!!!!!!!' He lets the last sound catch in his throat as he goes down on his haunches, in a crouching semi-foetal position. There's more whooping from the audience as he goes into a long, speedy diatribe about gardening, and road-testing popular pets, with all the requisite innuendo. He mentions the names of a few other TV celebs in passing. He stalks the stage like a televangelist, gesturing to the audience and at the roof with big sweeping motions. The crowd hoots and hollers encouragement.

'You tell 'em, boy!'

'Go, you good thing, *go*!'

'Put a *gap* in 'em!'

At the end, he raises both arms and takes a dramatic bow, knocking the microphone on his leg and causing a high-pitched feedback whistle. The audience goes sick as he steps down from the stage, handing the mike to the MC, a dark-haired woman in a paisley summer dress and a black cardigan.

'Thanks once again to Jason Pascoe!' she calls, and the applause gets louder for a moment before dying back to murmurs of enthusiasm. 'We're going to take a break before the open mike. In the meantime, you can buy beer and raffle tickets. We'll draw the raffle after the break. Thanks.' She puts the mike back on its stand and wanders off to a table filled with confident-looking people dressed in black, laughing happily and patting Jason Pascoe on the back.

'Good, hey?' asks Wayne.

'Yeah. Funny guy. Hey—are you going to go in the open mike?'

'Already put my name down.'

'What are you going to do?'

'I brought a couple, but I thought I'd try out a new one.'

A guy and a girl walk over and say hi to Wayne. The girl seems vaguely familiar.

'Kyle, Emma, this is Steven. Steven, Kyle and Emma.'

We shake hands. Kyle nods and smiles. Emma looks at me for a moment and then says, 'How's your knee?'

I stare at her blankly, feeling my knee with one hand. 'Fine?'

She laughs. 'We met at Melbourne Uni last year. Some guy knocked you down at the lights on Swanston Street. You were wearing green Converse high-tops.'

Oh my god. It's the cute Stereolab T-shirt girl. 'Ah. Sorry, I'm really crap with faces.'

She sits down next to me.

'Don't worry about it. I've got a good memory for that kind of thing.'

'So it seems.' Stay calm, I tell myself. Don't go all serendipitous on yourself just yet. Coincidences happen all the time, and most of the time they're not actually omens. Just be nice and friendly and let things take care of themselves. But of course I'm already over-thinking the situation, so I keep quiet and take a mouthful of beer while I try to work out how to keep her sitting here long enough for me to work out how to convey the impression of a funny, charming and sexy individual, to keep her sitting here even longer.

'You were wearing a Stereolab T-shirt,' I offer lamely.

She nods.

'It was a nice T-shirt.'

She smiles. I think I can see her eyes flicking around. I'm losing her.

'Red. With silver, right?'

She smiles and nods. 'Do you like Stereolab?'

Now what? Pretend that I do and risk making a dick of myself, or answer honestly and put an abrupt end to the conversation? I try the middle path. 'I haven't heard too much of their stuff. Used to live with someone who was a big fan, but I only really liked one album—Martian Audio something?'

'Mars Audiac Quintet?'

'Yeah, I liked it. Good background music.'

'It is,' she says. 'I made up a tape of my favourite songs of theirs. I take it out on road trips where I can kick the engine up to a hundred and twenty and wind the windows down and sing along at the top of my voice.'

'You know the words? I'm impressed.'

She grins. 'Like I said, good memory.'

'Okay, we're back with the raffle draw, and then we'll start the open mike.' Cardigan girl is back onstage. She pulls raffle tickets out of the inverted head of a giant plastic kewpie doll. A bottle of wine, a bunch of books and an assortment of crappy kids' toys are doled out to the appropriate ticket-holders, who squeal with delight as they run up to collect their prizes.

Wayne looks despondently at his tickets. 'I never fucking win anything,' he mutters. 'Another drink?' He wanders off to the bar.

Kyle nabs his seat, and leans forward on the table. 'You a poet, too, Steven?'

'Me? I just came here to see Wayne. How about you guys?'

'I write a bit of poetry,' says Emma.

'Guilty as charged,' says Kyle, frowning in mock disgust.

'So are you going up tonight?'

'I'm not,' says Emma. 'I haven't written anything new in a while.'

'I'm thinking about it,' says Kyle. 'Do you know if Wayne's up for it?'

'Yeah, he is. Can't imagine him turning down an opportunity to perform.'

'So, what do you do?' asks Emma.

I lean back in my chair and watch the first poet take the stage, an older guy in a faded brown suit. He reads a short rhyming poem about his mother and gets down to moderate applause.

'I work with Wayne at the post office.'

Wayne returns with three beers. 'Hey, you'll never guess who's here. Duncan Armstrong.'

'No way! I thought he was still up north. Where is he?' asks Kyle.

Wayne points over in the direction of the bar. Kyle jumps out of his seat and strides over to a man with thick blond dreadlocks and a tattered army jumper.

'Who's Duncan Armstrong?'

'Oh, he's a friend we haven't seen for a while.'

On stage, a woman intones from a black book that she holds up close to her face.

'So what do you do when you're not delivering mail?'

'Just stuff, I guess. Go shopping, watch TV, go out drinking, that sort of thing. I draw comics sometimes.'

'Really? What kind?'

Wayne leans over the table. 'Weird ones. All mythological symbolism and very little in the way of actual punch lines.'

'Some people,' I say, jerking my head in Wayne's direction, 'don't really understand what I'm trying to do with it.'

A woman dressed entirely in purple velvet gets up onstage. I remember her from the last time I came to see Wayne read. She had read a poem about a dead ex-lover. I recognise the words as she begins to read—it's the same poem.

'It's about three Gods from Indian mythology, only it's not really them. It's like they're the baby ones, sort of.'

'Ah,' says Emma, nursing her beer in the crook of her arm.

I'm hitting my stride. 'Yeah, I really got into the Hindu gods at Uni. I did this one course on myths and symbols in literature, to get away from psychology, and the units on the Indian gods sucked me right in.'

Emma sips her beer and looks at me. I'm babbling. I stop, but the silence makes me nervous so I jump straight in again. 'Yeah, so it's like they're the baby ones, except I've made two of them girls as well, because I thought there were too many boys in the stories like the Ramayana . . .'

'They sound . . . interesting.'

'I've got copies of them in my bag if you want.'

She smiles. 'You just happen to have them.'

I grab my bag and rummage around. This isn't going so badly after all. I remind myself to watch out for the usual trap of talking too much about myself. Remember to ask about her poetry, I tell myself. Ask her why she hasn't been writing lately. Ask her what she does for a job. Just ask about her, okay?

I hand Emma my copy of the latest *Zines, She Wrote* and resist the urge to tell her to turn to the middle pages. She's a bright individual—she'll work it out for herself. I keep my mouth shut and watch the poets.

A bearded guy does a rant about late-night television infomercials, which seems a little obvious to me. He's followed by a woman who attempts to categorise her former lovers in terms of body hair, height and tendency to leave the toilet seat up. Next comes a girl in a beanie who reads a poem about the mystical nature of cows. In between each act, Cardigan-girl jumps onstage and encourages the audience to clap louder, and to scream out 'Virgin!' at people who are reading for the first time.

Most of the crowd was here the last time I came. Most of the performers are the same ones I heard last time. And most of the performers are the same people who make up most of the crowd.

Wayne sits another three beers on the table. 'I think we lost Kyle for the night,' he says. 'I saw him heading out the front with Dunc.'

'They've probably gone to score,' says Emma, not looking up.

'Do you reckon it's easier to read in front of a bunch of poets, or a bunch of non-poets?' I ask.

'Poets. Definitely.'

'Yes, poets,' says Emma. 'Non-poets actually listen. It's a tougher gig all round. You have to be on.'

Ask about her, ask about her. 'You said you hadn't written anything new for a while. Why's that?'

'I tend to write in bursts, when I've got a strong idea.'

We empty our glasses and watch the barefooted hippy girl on stage chanting about victory in the rainforests.

'Next up tonight,' says Cardigan-girl, 'is a regular Friday night performer, Wayne Jackson.'

'Shit, that's me,' says Wayne. Emma and I applaud loudly as he takes the stage.

'This one's about . . . well, you'll get what it's about when I read it.' Wayne holds the microphone in both hands in his usual lead-singer style. I'm finding it hard to concentrate with Emma sitting right next to me, reading my comic. She tucks a loose strand of hair behind her ear and her mouth twitches. Was that a smile? I think that was a smile.

'They're good,' she says. 'I like the monkey.'

'Thanks.' My voice cracks slightly. She likes my comics. She likes my comics.

Wayne slaps me on the back as he takes his seat. 'What 'dja think?'

'Oh, yeah, really good,' I say. 'Funny.' I won't have to go into any detail if I compliment him. I stand up. It's my round. I need a short walk to clear my head after the pretty girl told me she liked my comics.

'No Anthea tonight?' I say to Wayne.

'We're still having communication problems.'

'Ah. Beer didn't work then, I take it.'

Wayne shrugs.

'You still shagging around, Wayne?' asks Emma. She looks at me and smiles. I like her style.

'So,' I say. 'When you *are* writing poetry, what kind of stuff do you write about?'

'I was writing one about Krazy Kat the other day, but it's not really finished.'

'Hang on—Krazy Kat? You mean the comic strip?'

'Yeah. You know it?'

'Know it? I love it! What's your poem about?'

'It was from the view of the bricks that Ignatz throws. How do they feel about being the messengers of love or hate? How do they feel about the ambiguity of their intention?'

'Hang on,' interrupts Wayne. 'I'm not following this.'

'It's this old 1920s comic strip called Krazy Kat, with two Ks,' I tell Wayne. 'There's this mouse called Ignatz and this cat called Krazy.'

'And Offisa Pup,' adds Emma. 'Krazy loves Ignatz, but Ignatz doesn't love Krazy, so he throws bricks at her to make her go away. Except that Krazy loves it when Ignatz hits her with a brick. Cartoon hearts start floating around her head. It was e.e.cummings's favourite comic strip.'

I'm starting to feel a little drunk and a little crushed, as in 'I think I'm developing a crush on this Stereolab-loving-good-memory-Krazy-Kat-poet woman'. Or maybe I'm just drunk. Fuck it. It can be two things.

'And Offisa Pup is the policeman dog who doesn't approve of Krazy and Ignatz's relationship. He keeps throwing Ignatz in for konking Krazy's caboose,' Emma continues.

'It's a surreal social-commentary kind of strip,' I add. 'There was one episode where Krazy found this extra-strong catnip called "Tiga Tee" . . .'

'That's one of my favourites,' says Emma.

'It's kind of a drug reference thing—anyone who drinks the Tiga Tee gets all loud and boisterous and beats everyone up, like they're on drugs or something.'

Wayne just sits there, nodding. 'Uh-huh. Do you have any of these at your place, Steve?'

'No, they're too rare.'

'I've got copies,' says Emma, sitting back smugly.

I do a double-take. 'Really? Oh, man. Would it—would it be all right if I came around and read them some time?' As soon as I say it, I realise how it sounds. Wayne grins, like the bastard he is.

Emma pauses and looks at me for a moment. 'Sure.' Then she empties her glass and asks if we're up for another round.

'Cute, isn't she?' says Wayne.

'Shut up.'

'Keep up the cartoon sweet-talk and she'll be asking you to throw bricks at her, man.'

'Shut *up*, Wayne.' The last thing I need right now is to get any more self-conscious.

Some time later we're sprawled all over the plush red couches at the back of the room. Various poets have joined us in our endeavour to get kicked out of the place. Two of them are musicians, who tell me the name of their band for the third time, and I forget it immediately. Something that sounds like 'parsley'.

Emma sets two bottles in front of us. 'That's last drinks, guys,' she says to the mob assembled on the couches. I look around. The rest of the place is pretty much empty apart from the woman behind the bar, who is talking to someone perched on a barstool, chain-smoking and fiddling with the stem of their wineglass.

I lean forward and grab the beer. My fingers curl around the cold glass and all of a sudden I find myself reluctant to lean back on the couch again. I'm more comfortable right here, with one hand on the beer and my elbows in my lap. I close my eyes and listen to the pulsing of blood through my body as it provides a bass line for the conversations going on around me. Wayne is talking about Bukowski, like he always does when he's drunk. Emma is talking about someone who's maybe had too much to drink. His name's Steven. I open my eyes and sit up straight.

'I'm okay,' I smile.

'You sure?'

I nod and lean back on the headrest. 'Yeah. I'm just a little tired. End of the week and all that, you know. Been awake for . . . what time is it now?'

'About a quarter to two.'

'Almost twenty-one hours.'

'Uh-oh,' says Emma.

'What?'

'That's a long time to be awake.'

'I think I might skip that last beer.'

'Good idea.'

I frown in mock anger. 'Are you saying I'm drunk?'

She laughs. A little pinging starts in my chest. I made her laugh. Have I done that yet tonight? I think so, maybe, yeah. But I made her laugh again. That's good. The pinging becomes a feeling like whisky warming the chest.

She rests her hand on my shoulder and looks at me, feigning sincerity. 'Would I do something like that?'

'I don't know. Would you?'

She leans back and closes her eyes for a moment. 'Actually, I think I've probably had enough, too. I'm going to head home.'

The whisky in my chest turns to ice. She's going home. I should ask for her phone number. That would be a reasonable thing to do. Now or never. Ask. And then, out of some parallel dimension that hasn't even been hypothesised yet by superstring theory, I hear my voice, a little softer than it's been all night, and a little meeker too. 'Emma? Um, would— would it be all right if I, if I came home with you?'

What the fuck? You were just going to ask for her phone number! What about plans and strategies and stuff? Calm down. You've had a great evening with a really cool woman who likes comics, for god's sake. You made her laugh. The two of you have been talking all night, about comics and Indian gods and poetry. You've got a—what's it?—a *rapport*. There's been physical contact of an implicatory nature and one or two meaningful moments of eye contact, that's all. Put the nervous costume away, boy, it's time to be a grown-up and ask for what you want. It's the only way to find out if you can have it. So shut up.

Then I hear Emma say, 'Okay', and inside my chest there's some kind of party that feels a bit like open-heart surgery. It's that easy? All you have to do is ask? Why didn't anyone tell me that before? A whole new world opens out in front of me, where I'm a superhero with the ability to ask girls if I can go home with them. What power! Can I handle the responsibility? Before I can freak out any further I shut down every part of my brain that could interfere with the excellent way tonight is working out. The whole thing takes less than a second, and at the end I'm the calmest, nicest, maturest man in the whole goddamn city and I don't even care that maturest isn't a word.

What the hell, might as well go for broke. I lean forward to kiss her.

First kiss make it good first kiss make it good first kiss make it good. Shut *up*!

It's gentle. She smells like roses and she tastes like beer. I probably taste like beer too, but I'm not sure what I smell like. I hope it's not rubber bands. I don't think that's a good first-kiss smell. I put one arm around Emma's shoulder and breathe deeply, inhaling the scent of her hair and her throat, feeling the softness of her jumper over the firmness of her shoulders. She slowly breaks contact and leans back. I look into her eyes and try not to grin too widely, in case my head splits open. The cute poet girl let me kiss her. How cool is that? She tilts her head and reaches out to me, placing one hand on the back of my neck and pulling me close. Our foreheads touch. I close my eyes.

'You gotta love the inhibition-releasing capacity of alcohol,' I say, and it comes out half as a slur, half a whisper.

'Mmmm,' she replies. We stay as we are for a while.

'We're going,' Emma announces to the group.

I nod, watching each person's face for reactions. It's all friendly smiles, especially from Wayne, who gives a not-so-subtle thumbs-up. I catch his eye and frown.

'Nice meeting you all. See you Monday, Wayne.'

Emma bends down to kiss a girlfriend goodbye on the cheek before leaving. I follow her out to find a taxi.

Emma rummages in her bag for her keys. I stand quietly beside her. Even though the ice is broken I'm still awkward about how to behave. I want to hug her, hold her hand maybe, but we're strangers. Strangers who have kissed, sure, but still strangers. I try to maintain a balance between politeness and drunken intimacy. I keep my hands in my pockets.

She flicks on the hall light and grabs for my hand, pulling me into the first room on the right. She sits down on the bed and looks at me, smiling and saying nothing. I'm nervous again. It's always weird being the stranger invited into someone's house. You could be anyone, and sometimes you find yourself being more polite than normal. It's refreshing to notice that I haven't lost my ability to over-analyse a situation. Realising that I am in prime form to say ridiculous things and only ridiculous things, I keep my mouth shut and sit down next to Emma. We kiss again. She still smells like roses. She shifts around so that she's kneeling on the bed in front of me, arms around my waist. I move my lips to her throat and she lifts her head back. She loses her balance and falls into me. I put my arms around her shoulders and we fall sideways, lying the length of the bed.

Hands trace the curve of bodies, sneak under shirts, between legs, fumble with clasps and zippers. Tongues touch. Warm breath caresses skin. We slide out of our clothes and under the covers. I am overwhelmed by the sensation of her skin against my skin and I try not to step outside myself, try to focus on the sensations of my body coming into contact with Emma's body. I almost succeed. The voice inside my head is on overdrive, but I manage for the most part to ignore it. Somewhere between freaking out about the fact that the first time I ever make a move it works out this well, and laughing hysterically about something I'll have forgotten by the morning (though I won't have forgotten that laughing with Emma is something I want to do a lot more of); somewhere between Emma rummaging in her underwear drawer for condoms and trying to work out exactly how drunk I am, we manage to have sex. We manage to have sex, and I think it's pretty good for first-time sex. I mean, I like it, sure. I have an excellent time, but really you'd have to interrupt me right now and tell me that not only have all my family died in a car accident but that I have to spend the rest of my life in a Malawian jail with ten convicted rapists after having my eyes put out by a red-hot poker—you'd have to tell me something along those lines, but a bit more serious, to even begin to dampen my mood at the point where I sigh in Emma's arms and she twists around so that I'm holding her with my chest against her back, my arms tucked under her breasts, her wrists held gently in my hands, my face against her neck, spooning as I fall asleep smelling her hair and feeling the texture of these not-mine sheets as they trap the warmth of our bodies around us. I like it, sure, but I think Emma liked it too, and that thought, despite the point and counterpoint and commentary and self-analysis resounding in my head, is enough to allow me one of the calmest nights of sleep I can remember.

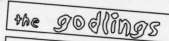

the godlings

SATURDAY

I wake with my back curled against Emma.

'Sleep well?' She's already awake.

There are a million dumb things to say at this moment, but I hold them back. 'Mmmmm . . .'

She rolls over to face me. I turn to face her.

'You snored.'

'Sorry,' I say, trying to look less embarrassed than I feel. Snoring. Not sexy. Kind of gross. Oops.

'Just a little. You were very quiet,' she says, with a smirk. 'I gave you a nudge and you stopped. It's okay. I snore too.'

'I didn't notice.'

'Well, you can't drink that much and not snore, can you?' She moves forward and kisses me. It tastes nice. I kiss back. We kiss for a while and then she moves closer, cupping her hand around me. I feel the warmth of her breasts against my chest, the firmness of her shoulders, the softness of her skin. I hook one leg over hers and slide my arms around her back. This time it's less frenzied, which is good, because despite how wonderful it is to be half-asleep and naked and doing this right now,

I can feel a nascent hangover between my eyes and I don't think I'd be able to match last night's performance in terms of reckless abandon. Emma reaches under the pillow and passes me another condom. I raise my eyebrows in surprise, and as she pushes her tongue into my mouth she murmurs that she found it in her sock drawer. My first thought is to howl with joy at the fact that she went looking for a second condom, which must mean she likes me enough to sleep with me again. My second thought is 'well, duh' as I remember where I am.

The sex is gentle and lucid. Last night we were breaking down inhibitions. This morning we're shyly saying hello with our entire bodies. There's a nervous energy to it that makes me think maybe I won't need any painkillers today—maybe the endorphins and the adrenalin and the sheer pleasure of this encounter will keep the hangover at bay.

Afterwards we lie in each other's arms and continue our get-to-know-you conversations. We swap middle names, high-school crushes and favourite comics. Emma gets out of bed and I watch her move around the room as she searches for something. She comes back with the Krazy Kat book we talked about last night.

'Read it later,' she says. I put it to one side as she moves in for another kiss. Eventually we break the clinch, and our lazy hung-over conversation drifts around to jobs. Emma talks about how much she hates her current job, temping in an office in the city, but I trump her with my story about the recent traumas on my run.

'Man bites dog,' she says.

'What?'

'It's the test for newsworthiness. Dog bites man—that's something that you'd expect to happen, so it's not news. But man bites dog—that's unusual. That's news.'

'But I didn't bite Satan,' I say. 'He tried to bite me.'

'Why chicken? Wouldn't something like—I don't know—sausages or a handful of mince be cheaper?'

'I guess. I never thought about it before. Wayne said "chicken", so I got chicken.'

The alarm clock on the bedside table says twelve-fifteen. We've slept and snuggled and fucked the morning away.

'I should probably get going soon.'

'Yeah, I have a few things to do today,' says Emma.

I make an effort to sit up. My head doesn't fall off or implode, so I figure that's a good sign. I could use some water, though. And I need to take a piss.

'Do you want a shower?'

I do want a shower, but there's the whole housemate thing to take into consideration. I don't know if Emma lives alone or not, or if her house-mates are awake and moving around at the moment, but I'd rather avoid bumping into them right now. It's always awkward being 'the stranger that so-and-so brought home last night'. I don't think I'm up for the polite nods and the surreptitious exchange of knowing glances that comes with the situation. 'Um, no thanks. I'll just have one when I get home.'

'You sure?'

'Yeah, thanks.'

'You smell like a goat, you know.'

I stare at her.

'Because of the sex,' she whispers in a stage mock-whisper.

Goat? Is that an insult or intimacy? 'Uh . . .'

'And so do I, which is why *I'm* going to have a shower.' She slides out of bed, shrugs into a black satin robe with Chinese embroidery on the back, and pads out of the room.

Now what do I do? I'm lying naked and sex-stained in a stranger's bedroom—what's the appropriate response? Should I be here when she comes back? Was she giving me some kind of hint? Should I just get dressed and sneak out the front door now? Leave a note? I wanted to kiss her goodbye. I think about our lips touching and decide that, yes, I definitely want to kiss her goodbye, so that means I'll wait here until she finishes her shower. Maybe I can do a little victory dancing while she's out of the room. I jump onto the floor and wiggle my hips, then do a bit of hip-hop posturing. Oh *yeah*. Look at *me*. I just had *sex. Twice.* To the *beat* y'all.

That feels better. I stand still and look around the room. Lots of book-shelves. Lots of books. Emma's got a good comics library here. I flick through a couple, but I'm not in a reading mood. I check out the shelf underneath and a slim spine catches my eye. *You and What Army?* by Emma Monori. Monori? I wonder if that's Emma. A quick look at the photo on the back cover confirms that it is her. It's weird that you can know what the back of someone's knee tastes like, but not know their surname. I jump under the doona and start reading.

It's different from Wayne's poetry. More like I expect poetry to be, but still conversational—like song lyrics that tell a story. It's not all about everyday life. There's a poem about skinning a horse, another one about superhero sidekicks, and a couple based on primary school games like scarecrow chasey and those old skipping-rope rhymes. 'Hide and Seek' is a longish poem about a girl hiding from her boyfriend in weirder and weirder places. The last few lines catch my eye.

Now I'm here, resting quietly between the folds of
your brain, mesmerised by the arc and shimmer of
your neurons in action. I knew you had a remarkable mind,

but it's another thing entirely to watch synapses hiss
and crackle as you seek me out, piecing together
the clues I left for you. It won't be long now.

This time, though, things will be different.
This time, when you find me, I plan to stay found.

I think it's a love poem, but it's full of weird things from science fiction B-movies. A B-movie love poem. How cool is that? I would have said that laser guns and long-lost loves had nothing to do with each other, but Emma's poetry seems to suggest otherwise. That's a remarkable brain she's carrying around in that head of hers.

Emma comes back with her water-darkened hair plastered against her neck. I look up, feeling a little guilty.

'Where'd you find that?'

'In the bookshelf.'

She pauses, looking at me, almost frowning. 'Had a bit of a rummage, did we?'

'I was looking for comics.' I sound more apologetic than I mean to, so I clear my throat.

'It's fine. Teasing.' She closes the door behind herself. 'I was wondering if you'd be here when I got back.'

I check to see if there's a clue here as to whether I made the right choice in staying, but I can't tell. 'I like your poems,' I say, changing the subject. 'They're really . . . nice.' 'Nice'? Excellent. I sound like a moron. 'I mean they're . . . clever.' Oh, much better. A round of applause for the nonverbal dork here.

'Thanks.' She drops the robe around her ankles and climbs back into bed. I shuffle over to make room, trying to keep a respectful but naked distance. 'It's a bit old, all that stuff.'

I hand the book to her. She rolls onto her side and throws it over her shoulder. 'I put it out about four years ago. I've still got a box of them under my bed.'

'You made it yourself? Wow.'

'What?'

'It just looks really . . . professional. It's not stapled.'

'Perfect binding's a bit more expensive, but you want people to be able to see it on a bookshelf. I got a friend to help with the design. You want one?'

'I'll buy one from you.'

'Pfft. Don't be stupid,' she reaches under the bed, comes back up with a copy of the book and tosses it at me.

'Thanks.' I look over at the clock, but the time doesn't register. 'I should probably get going.'

I find my underpants in a pile with my T-shirt and jeans. Where did I throw my socks? What colour socks was I wearing? I check under the bed and find two black socks that I assume are mine. 'Did you see where I put my shirt?'

'Over on the chair.'

I finish dressing and sit on the edge of the bed to tie my shoes, then lean over to kiss her. 'Thanks for a wonderful night.' I feel cheesy for delivering such a crappy line, but I'm unable to come up with anything cleverer. 'And for the book,' I add, holding it up like it's a prize and I'm posing for the cameras. Dork.

'You're welcome.'

'Um—can I call you some time?' I ask. The lines are getting cheesier, but I'm still at a loss. Maybe there is no cool way to do this.

'Sure,' she says. She grabs a thick black texta from the bedside table and writes her phone number on the palm of my hand. She underlines it and writes her name in capitals. It tickles. 'Careful, you'll smudge it,' she says, tightening her grip.

When she's done she hands me the texta and holds out her hand. I put my hands on her shoulders, push her onto the bed and lie across her belly, pinning her down. She squeals and struggles as I scrawl my phone number on her arm in big black numbers. She screams at me to stop, and I laugh and scream back, telling her to hold still.

'If you move too much you'll end up with someone else's phone number, and you'll never be able to find me again.'

'I will be able to!' she yells. 'I'll just follow the smell of GOAT!'

I dive into her neck and start kissing her all over, sticking my tongue in her ear and pinching her knees under the doona. She laughs as she struggles, almost throwing me off. I'm laughing too, blowing raspberries on her belly and running my fingers along her arms. It occurs to me that I might be exceeding the bounds of guy-who-just-met-you-last-night with this playfighting shtick. I pause to consider this, and at that moment Emma bucks upward and I'm off the bed, lying on my back thinking that however much fun this kind of ruckus is, it's probably best done without having drunk copious amounts of beer the night before. I lie still, feeling the blood pounding in my head as I catch my breath. All I can see is the ceiling and the side of the bed. Emma comes into view as she pokes her head over where I'm lying.

'Are you okay?' she asks.

I exhale dramatically. 'Sure,' I say. 'Just relaxing for a minute.'

'I was going to get you a piece of *paper*,' she says. 'Now I have to have another shower.'

I slowly climb to my feet. 'I should leave you to it, then.' I step forward and kiss her again. This could go on all afternoon.

'Okay,' she says, with a smile.

'Okay,' I say.

We break contact. I grab my jacket from the foot of the bed.

'Bye.'

'Bye.' I like the lilt in her voice when she says this. To my sex-sated mind it holds promise of future encounters.

Emma snuggles back under her doona. I don't want to leave, but I think I need some time alone to process the events of the last few hours.

I close the front door quietly behind me and look around for landmarks. I spot the skyscraper with the angled roof and realise that I'm not far from the Victoria Market. I can walk into the city and catch a tram home from there.

I only make it past three houses before there's a skip in my step and I'm shaking my booty to the groove in my mind and shooting imaginary guns into the air, dancing the victory dance all the way into the city and composing a poem to fit the occasion.

'Made the first MOO-oove.

Got to have SE-ex . . .

With a pretty GIR-irrl . . .

Word to yo MAMA . . .'

The phone ringing in the hallway resolves out of my dream and into reality. I swim slowly up to consciousness, disoriented. My doona is heavy and stifling. I feel cooling sweat on my forehead. The ringing stops at the click of the answering machine.

'Hi. You've called Van and Steven. We're either out somewhere or sitting next to the phone to determine whether you're someone we want to talk to. Take your chances and leave a message.'

'Steven? It's Gina. Pick up if you're screening.'

I stay where I am, unconvinced that waking up is the best thing for me right now.

'Okay. It's just gone seven—I'll meet you round the back of the vet's in half an hour, okay? I need to check something out. We'll do Rae Street later on. Call me if you can't make it. Bye.'

The stake-out. I'd forgotten about that. I pull one arm out from under the doona and rest it on my chest. I open my eyes to the dimness of my bedroom and assess my physical status.

My tongue feels furry and I can taste the distinctly chemical tang of the burger I scarfed on the way home as a hangover cure. I burp quietly. Yep, there it is. The unmistakable taste of whatever they claim is onion in onion rings. On the positive side, while I feel dehydrated, there's not much of a headache to this hangover. I sit up gingerly and reach for the bottle of water on my bedside table. The water goes some way towards eliminating the skanky fast-food taste. I scratch my head, then scratch my arse. The stake-out. Standing in the dark behind the vet's surgery with Gina for four hours, waiting patiently for something to happen, which it won't. It could be a fun night hanging out with Gina, if it wasn't for how serious she'll be, patiently waiting for the criminal to return to the scene of the crime, which they won't. I'll just have to stand there, freezing my tits off, until she decides we can go home. Or I could pretend that I didn't get the message until it was too late, call her tomorrow and apologise, and in the meantime have a proper hung-over evening slobbing around the house watching crap TV and replaying the delicious events of last night in my mind. Not a tough decision, really.

I make a concession to fair play and resolve that if Gina comes around or calls me again I'll cop it sweet and do the stake-out with her, but until then I'll just lie back and get some more sleep.

My head easily finds its place in the pillow, and I'm just settling down to generate a generous quantity of beta-waves when the phone rings again. I hate it when my moral fortitude is tested.

I slump out of bed and shuffle to the phone. 'Hello?'

'You sound like shit.' It's Wayne.

I clear my throat. 'I just got out of bed.'

'I bet you did.'

'And what exactly is that supposed to mean?'

'I think you know.'

'Yeah, yeah.'

'So, how was it? I mean, did you have fun? I mean, is she . . . nice?'

'Yeah, yeah she's great. Really smart. I like her.'

'And a good kisser, yeah?'

'Wayne.'

'Just asking.'

'I know you are.'

'Well anyway, you broke the drought. Yowsa.'

'I don't know if I'd call it a drought.'

'I would.'

'Compared to you, Wayne, everybody's experiencing a drought.'

'You flatter me.'

'Not as much as you do.'

'Anyway, what are you up to tonight?'

'Not much, why?'

'I'm heading out to the Nape with Kyle and Duncan and that. Wondered if you wanted to come along.'

'Nah, thanks all the same but I don't think more alcohol is what's required here. I think I'll just stay home tonight and veg out. Maybe get an early one.'

'Saturday night, mate. You're not old yet.'

'All the same . . .'

'Okay. If you change your mind we'll be there 'til close.'

'Cool. Seeya.'

I shuffle back into my bedroom, flick the light on and look around. The pile of Godlings strips is sitting in the printer tray. I read one. Seems like everyone I know has made their own book. Wayne and Gina, and now Emma. They all make it look easy. All I need to do is staple these twenty pages together, add a cover and maybe some contact details, and it's a comic.

As I boot up the computer I notice Emma's phone number on the back of my hand, a bit faded from the hasty shower I had before collapsing into bed. I copy the number from my hand and pin the scrap of paper to my notice board. Maybe I'll call her later tonight. Is that too keen? No, it's polite. I'll ring her and say thanks for last night and see if she wants to catch up again soon. Yeah, that's what I'll do. I'll design a cover and then I'll make the call.

I make a strong coffee, put King Missile on the stereo, crank it, head back to my room and open up Illustrator, then take a sip of coffee, feeling its caffeinated tendrils infiltrate my bloodstream with its unique blessings, and start working.

A couple of hours later I've got an eye-catching cover. It's an enlarged picture of Li'l Hanuman grinning her static grin as she mouths the words of a Britney Spears song. The image is taken from a strip inside, where she's bouncing around the other two shrieking the lyrics and generally pissing them off. 'Godlings', announces the banner heading, and below Hanuman is the legend 'volume 1. now with extra monkeys!'. It's nice. Simple, but nice. Best to keep it simple. I'll get fancier with the next issue.

Right now the point is to bang it down and get it out. I've also written a little introduction for the inside page, with a bio of each of the characters, and a sort of statement of intent about the Indian gods that they're based on. I think it looks pretty good. I stack the pages together and set them to one side. Now all I need to do is photocopy them. I'll ask Wayne where he does his.

Quarter to ten. Is that too late to call someone you don't know very well? Maybe I should wait until tomorrow. Maybe she's out tonight. It is Saturday night, after all. Maybe I should wait a couple of days before I call.

Stop it, I tell myself. It's just crush nerves. The best thing for crush nerves is to do exactly what you're nervous about doing. Someone told me that once. Might as well give it a go. I dial the number slowly and then wait. It's ringing. Will she be pissed off that I've called so late? Am I crowding her? Rushing her? Does she even want to have anything to do with me any more? Was last night just a one-night stand?

Someone's answered. It's a girl. Is it Emma? I don't know. It doesn't sound like Emma, but I've never heard her on the phone before.

'Um, hi. Emma?'

'No, she's out. Can I take a message?'

After the adrenalin surge of making the call, now that I'm not actually talking to Emma, I'm left feeling deflated and hung-over. 'Um, yeah. If you could. Can you just let her know that Steven called?' I try not to sound disappointed.

'Okay, does she have your number?'

'Yeah, she does. Thanks.'

As I hang up it occurs to me that maybe Emma doesn't have my number. Maybe she washed it off in the shower before she got a chance to write it down. But she'd already had a shower. Maybe she had another one before she went out. She said she would, but I have nothing to indicate what her hygiene habits are.

I look at the faint trace of Emma's number on my hand. Sure, it's still kind of visible, but maybe Emma uses stronger soap. Maybe she uses a loofah or a pumice stone or something. Should I call back and make sure she's got the number? Should I call back and ask if she exfoliates? Would her housemates know if she exfoliates? I know that Van exfoliates, because of the pumice stone that always falls off the ledge when I'm in the shower.

Now I'm left hanging. If Emma doesn't have my number, how long should I wait before calling back again? Is tomorrow morning too soon? I'd forgotten about the mind-fuck aspect of crushes. Here I was thinking it'd be all roses and bunny rabbits and shit, completely forgetting the hair-shirt factor. I take a deep breath and head into the lounge. I flick on the TV and flump down on the couch. The Saturday night movie is starting. I decide to let my hung-over brain devolve completely into mush with the aid of whatever Hollywood pap is on offer. I only hope it's not a romantic comedy. I don't think I could handle one of those right now.

Judging from the dark lighting, it's most likely some kind of action film. I watch, slack-jawed, as some guy sneaks in somewhere and steals something, and then some other guy comes up behind him and grabs him, throws him against a wall and shoots him. The credits start to roll. It's got Bruce Willis in it. That sounds okay. It's got Rip Torn, too. That'll be a laugh. I don't recognise any of the other names.

Twenty minutes in and my mind is truly pulped by the incomprehensibly simplistic chase movie that's unfolding before my eyes. The pulping is only exacerbated by the ad breaks, which I find myself watching with equal intensity. Not a good sign when you can't look away from the commercials. I struggle to avert my eyes.

I think about the comic I'm about to send off into the world. I imagine seeing it on bookshelves in bookshops. I imagine seeing it in comic shops. I imagine people flipping through it at the counter. Maybe someone famous or powerful will notice it. Maybe *Rolling Stone* will print my strips, and they'll become the latest fad, inspiring all manner of merchandising spin-offs: plush toys, stickers, action figures and computer games. Maybe Disney will offer to buy the rights and pay teenagers a pittance to climb inside sweat-stinking costumes based on my characters. Maybe a hit cartoon series will be developed, beamed into people's lounge rooms on Thursday prime-time evenings. Maybe brain-dead morons in shopping centres will hide their nakedness with T-shirts emblazoned with the grinning miens of Kid Shiva, Li'l Hanuman and Maitreya the Kid. Yeah, maybe. And maybe, to paraphrase the saying, monkeys with flaming tails will fly out of my arsehole.

Still, the promise of seeing the Godlings comic on the shelves in a couple of seedy bong-shops and filthy indie record stores is enticing. I wander to the kitchen to deal with the hangover munchies that have just kicked in. I settle for the easy solution: a toasted cheese sandwich with tomato sauce. I flick off the TV and head back to check my email. It's all crap. I log off and shut down, then tumble into bed to dream about Emma returning my call.

SUNDAY

Emma is standing on the front step with a red mountain bike leaning against her hip. She's wearing a loose green long-sleeved T-shirt and black tight-fitting shorts. Her hair is tied back underneath her helmet. I gulp.

'Ready to go?'

'Sure, just give me a second. Wanna come in?'

'Okay.'

She wheels her bike into the hallway and rests it up against the wall. I wander into my room and wait for her to follow. Should I have kissed her hello? She doesn't look disappointed that I haven't, but maybe she's just good at hiding it.

'Whatcha working on?'

'Just that comic I showed you with the Indian gods,' I say, stepping aside so that she can see the screen.

'Have you read Joseph Campbell?' she asks.

'Uh, no. He's the *Star Wars* guy, yeah?'

'I thought you studied mythology at university.'

'Sort of, yeah. I kind of stopped going after a couple of weeks,' I admit.

'The classes started at eight-forty-five a.m., and I never seemed to be able to get there on time . . .'

'Well, you would have done Campbell. He's a comparative mythologist. I think you'd like him.'

She looks around. I watch her taking it all in: the bookshelf crammed with comics, the Magritte prints Blu-tacked to the walls, the pile of dirty laundry on my bed. She turns to look at me and I lean forward to kiss her, but she moves away to check out the backwards-facing bowler-hat guy. I change the direction of my lunge and shut down the computer. I scratch the back of my neck, hoping she didn't notice what just happened.

'Should we get going?'

'Sure.' She flashes me a big smile.

My knees go weak. I clear my throat. 'I'll just go get my bike from the back.'

'Okay,' she says, stepping over a wet towel to inspect my comic shelf.

I wander out into the hallway, trying to work up the guts for another kiss. We've seen each other naked but I'm still nervous around her. Stupid crush nerves. I wheel my bike through the house and grab my helmet and backpack from beside the bed.

'All set?'

I sneak a peek at the comic she was looking at. *The Mystifying Adventures of Man-with-a-Monkey Man*. She's got good taste.

It's a gorgeous day outside—blue sky and enough sun to make your skin tingle.

'What's in the backpack?'

'I bought some stuff for the picnic—corn chips and Turkish bread. And dips.'

'Excellent,' she says, mounting her bike. 'You've never been to the children's farm before?'

'No.'

'Well, I thought we'd follow the Merri Creek trail.'

'Where's that?' I ask.

She laughs, then stops herself abruptly. 'How long have you been living in North Fitzroy?'

'About two years.'

'And you've never ridden along the creek.'

'No.'

'Where do you ride your bike then?'

I nudge my helmet back on my head. 'I don't know, along the streets, you know. My run. Through the parks. Canning Street. Into the city. Critical Mass. That sort of thing.' First I stuffed up the kiss and now she thinks I'm an idiot because I've never ridden along the creek. I'm not having much fun. I try to hide my sulk, but it's pretty obvious.

'Hey, it's okay,' Emma says, softening her tone. 'I'm just mucking around . . .'

I look up. 'I know, but I'm kind of nervous . . .'

'That's sweet.' She sounds amused. I feel dumb. Stupid crush nerves. She looks at me for a moment, her nose scrunched up and her eyes narrowed. I look into her eyes, trying to work out what it is she's looking at. She turns and mounts her bike. 'Come on.'

Emma takes the lead, riding down to St Georges Road, left and hard right at the bottle shop, then across the school crossing onto a cement path that goes under the railway bridge before coming out in a quiet suburban street full of brick houses with roses in their front yards. We turn right into a tree-lined street with sunlight flickering between the leaves. The street curves left, but Emma keeps going over a narrow bridge. I look down and see the sparkling water of Merri Creek. How good is this? How could I not have known this was here, only five minutes from my doorstep? A couple of ducks are paddling just below the bridge. I breathe deeply, sucking in the ionised air and washing my lungs clean.

We coast past willow trees and under a red-brick bridge. This is so cool, like a hidden country right in the middle of the city. The bike path twists and turns, cutting over the creek and back again on little wooden bridges that burr as our tyres cut across their surface. We slog up hills, breathing hard and standing on our pedals, then coast down the other side. We pass couples pushing babies in prams and families walking their dogs. We overtake joggers. I nod with the camaraderie of a fellow cyclist to the people riding in the opposite direction. Sometimes they nod back, sometimes they don't, but I don't care. I feel like I'm drinking in some kind of nectar, like the Merri Creek has got inside me somehow. I must have the biggest, dopiest grin on my face.

We follow the path until we come to a sign that says 'Collingwood Children's Farm', and ride under a wooden ramp, past bright-yellow traffic signs and between wooden fences. There's a chook shed on our left, and a wooden building with pigs in it. There are piles of hay everywhere. Little kids are poking their hands through wire fences to pat sheep on the other side. Parents are holding smaller kids on their hips and pointing out the geese. Horses stand nonchalantly in the back paddocks.

Emma slows down as we approach a group of people standing around in front of two goats. She dismounts and parks her bike. I slow and jump off too. Emma walks up to the goat-feeders, smiling and saying hello. 'Guys, this is Steve,' Emma says. 'Steve, this is Brianne, Jem, Dave, Carrie and Lace.'

I nod to the group. They all smile hello. I remember Lace from the pub, and I might have seen Carrie and Dave on stage that night. Brianne is familiar, too, but I'm not sure where I know her from.

'There's nowhere to have our picnic,' says Jem.

Emma bends down to pat the goat, but it shies away and nibbles grass on the edge of the path. She looks up at Jem. 'Let's follow the path up over the bridge, then,' she says.

'Okay, let's do it,' says Lace. 'I'm hungry.'

We grab our bikes and walk them past paddocks with farm animals, and a huge brick building that looks a bit like a church on our right, except there's a swimming pool in front of it. I stay quiet, still impressed by the presence of so much greenery so close to home.

'Pretty nice, hey?' Emma sidles up to me and matches her pace with mine.

'Uh-huh. I had no idea there was anything this pretty in Melbourne.'

'Well, now you do.'

I nod. 'So how are you, anyway?'

She smiles. 'Good. I had fun the other night.'

'Me too. It was really nice.' I pause. 'That sounds so lame, sorry. It's hard being clever when you're talking to a poet.'

Emma laughs and touches my arm. 'It *was* nice.'

We walk side by side in silence for a moment. 'So where do these guys fit in?' I ask.

'Well, Jem and I work together, Lace is an old friend from high school, Dave and Carrie I know from the poetry scene, and Brianne is Carrie's girlfriend.'

'Remind me what kind of work you do.'

'Temping in the city. Usually some kind of admin, sometimes reception work. Right now I'm a receptionist for a broker.'

'Oh. That sounds . . .'

'Boring?'

I laugh.

'Nowhere near as romantic as being a postie. Helping keep people in contact with the outside world, their friends, their loved ones . . .'

'The multinational corporations that they owe money to.'

She smiles and nudges my shoulder. I feel an internal buzzing start up. I wonder if she can hear it.

We find a flat, grassy area, dotted with tiny yellow and white flowers, and lay out our picnic of delicatessen delicacies. We descend on the food, passing bread and dips, dropping olives and mashing chip-crumbs into the blanket, then we lie back, sated, leaving the scraps to bake in the after-noon sunshine. I watch the clouds move across the sky as the sun sinks lower. Most people in the park have gone home now, but a few dogs and their owners are emerging for early evening walks.

'I went to Benjo's book launch the other night,' says Dave.

'How's the book look?'

'Okay, I guess. The author photo was all right.'

'Oh, you bitch.'

I'm lying on my back on the corner of the blanket, with Emma sitting on one side and Brianne on the other. I'm only vaguely following this conversation, never having met Benjo or read his poetry.

'Are you a poet?' Brianne asks me.

'No, I'm a postie.'

'That must be fun.'

'It has its moments. What about you? Are you a writer too?'

'Worse,' she grimaces. 'An actor.'

'That doesn't sound so bad.'

'You don't know many actors.'

'Um, no. So, do you do plays or . . .'

'Mostly theatre, but I've done a little bit of telly, too.'

'Anything I would have seen?'

She laughs quietly and tilts her head at me. 'Oh, I did some ads, one for a car company . . .'

'Yeah, I *thought* you looked familiar.' I remember the ad she's talking about. They've got her dressed up as some glam reporter-chick so she can ask the car questions. I think it's meant to be post-modern, but it's just crap, really. Wayne does a pretty good impersonation of her. I refrain from mentioning it. Better to play nice with Emma's friends. I want to make a good impression here.

'What else have you done?'

'Not much really. I just had an audition for a TV show.'

'Which one?'

'*The Secret Life of Us.*'

I grimace at the reference, then realise what I'm doing and try to hide it. Too late. She noticed.

'It's not much chop, I know,' she says apologetically, 'but it's regular work.'

'Not much chop?' says Jem. 'It's fucking terrible. I can't believe you want to be associated with it.'

'Well, you know.' Brianne rubs her fingers together in the universal sign for moolah.

Jem feigns indignation and falls backward.

'What shits me about it,' says Lace, 'is that it sets itself up as an accurate picture of the lives of people like us, when it's just another helping of soap-opera bullshit all about the day-to-day heartache of being a twenty-something in the big city. Throw in a bit of token homosexuality and there you go.'

'Well, it's been getting good reviews,' says Brianne, 'and the script I read was okay, not as bad as *Neighbours*.'

'Good reviews mean nothing,' says Lace. 'They're paid for.'

'I don't know—I met the producers and they seemed passionate about what they were doing, writing stories that haven't been told on television before and stuff.'

'Bullshit. All the hype is this "never been done before, gritty realism, something for young people to identify with", but all the characters they've written are vapid, self-absorbed dickheads.'

'Well, at least all the vapid, self-absorbed dickheads will have something to identify with,' says Emma.

'It sounds like *Home and Away* for grown-ups,' says Carrie.

'All television is *Home and Away* for grown-ups,' says Jem. 'That's why I only watch the ABC.'

'I thought *Home and Away* was *Home and Away* for grown-ups,' says Dave.

'It is,' says Brianne.

'Fucking wanker,' Lace says, throwing a dolmade at Jem, who catches it and puts it in his mouth. '"I only watch the ABC." Next you'll be telling us you only listen to Radio National.'

'NewsRadio, actually,' Jem says, grinning.

Lace throws the last dolmade at him and he ducks. A little dog runs up and scarfs it down.

'So, do you want the job?' I ask Brianne, watching the dog scarper.

'If they ask me back, I'll probably do it.'

'And then we'll finally realise our dreams of knowing someone *famous*,' says Dave. 'I always knew it would be you, Bree.'

Brianne sticks her tongue out at Dave, who returns the gesture with an upraised finger.

'I don't know why they even bother trying to make "realistic" drama series,' says Lace. 'Television is nothing like real life. Not even documentaries. It's all constructed. Even reality TV is fake. The cast of *Big Brother* were all actors. TV has nothing significant to offer other than entertainment for idiots.'

'Try telling that to my friend Gina,' I say. 'She's convinced that *Murder, She Wrote* will help clear my name.'

'Clear your name?' asks Brianne.

'It's a long story.'

'We love long stories,' says Dave.

'All right,' I say and launch into the story of Satan's death once again. The whole thing sounds more like a stupid urban legend each time I tell it, except that it isn't something I heard from a friend of a friend.

'Anyway, after the body disappeared Gina decided that we should stake out the old lady's house and the vet's clinic to see if whoever took the body . . . shit. What time is it?'

Carrie looks at her watch. 'Twenty to six, why?'

I close my eyes. I've done it again. 'I was supposed to meet Gina at four today. We were going to stake out the vet's. Fuck.'

'Oops,' says Lace.

I roll over onto my stomach. 'Big oops. This is the second time I've stood her up.' I sigh. 'Oh, well. I'll call her tonight and explain.'

'What do you do on your stake-outs?' asks Carrie.

'Not much. Sit in the car. Stare at a house across the street. It's not very exciting.'

'The death of Satan,' says Lace. 'How very Nietzschean.'

'I'm getting cold. Maybe we should head back,' says Emma.

'We were thinking of catching a film,' says Carrie.

'Yeah, maybe,' Emma says. 'Wanna come, Steve?'

I look over at Emma, who is clipping the lids back on the dried-up dip containers. Gee. Do I want to spend the rest of the night hanging out with the girl I'm smitten with at the moment, and who might even ask me back to her place later tonight? I wonder.

The orange light of Victoria Street bathes us as we cycle past the Victoria Market. We follow the tramlines west until we hit Emma's street, then hang a right and slide to a stop in front of her house. I'm quiet as I follow Emma through to the yard and prop my bike next to hers.

Jem and Lace had chosen an obscure Iranian film, and afterwards they'd sat around discussing it over oily pizza and strong coffee. I let the others do most of the talking. They claimed to see whole levels of meaning that I hadn't noticed, changing my opinion of the film from boring desert coming-of-age story to something I'd maybe watch on SBS if I was home by myself and there weren't any cartoons or science fiction or game shows on. I spent most of the conversation watching Emma, admiring the curve of her throat as it descended towards her collarbone and the way her dark eyes flicked from person to person as she listened to their points of view. I was trying to work out how to bring up the question of coming home with her. Was it better to assume that I was invited, or to corner her and ask? I realised that the decision had been made for me when Emma stood up, pushing her chair back with a scraping sound.

'Coming?' she asked.

I nodded, aiming for a balance between enthusiastic and nonchalant. Stupid crush nerves.

I go through the hallway and kitchen and into the lounge room. Emma is already sitting on the couch, her feet up on the coffee table. I sit down next to her. I look around, still a little nervous and perplexed at my inability to relax around her. 'Your friends are really nice,' I say. There's that word again.

'Yeah, they're okay.'

'They seem pretty smart and with it.'

'They're just good bullshit artists—not even that good, actually. They really get on my nerves sometimes, all this cooler-than-thou stuff, bagging out that TV show just because it's popular at the moment. They always have to be one step ahead of everyone else. If people like it, it must be crap. I get sick of it sometimes.'

'Oh.' I'm not sure what to say now. I feel dumb again, which seems to be happening a lot these days. It's nice to know that Emma's smarter than her try-hard friends, though. Makes me like her even more.

'I don't know, maybe I'm just getting too old for that kind of hipster lifestyle. I used to hang shit on trends with the rest of them, but after a few years it just gets . . . *boring.*'

'How old are you?'

'Twenty-seven.'

'Oh.'

'What do you mean, "oh"? How old did you think I was?'

'I don't know . . . my age? Maybe a year older?'

'How old are you?'

'Twenty-two.'

'Ah.'

'What do you mean, "ah"?'

She pulls me towards her and kisses me gently, running her tongue around my lips and into my mouth. She pulls back for a second to look me in the eye and whisper, 'Nothing.'

She kisses me again and we sit on the couch, snogging like teenagers for a while. Eventually we stop and sit in silence. Twenty-seven? I've slept with an older woman? Holy shit.

'So how come you're hanging out with a twenty-two year old, then?' I ask. 'Shouldn't you be seeing someone more your age?'

'Who says I'm not?'

I freeze like I've just been shot at. How the fuck do I respond to that one?

'So what are you going to tell your friend about today?' Emma asks.

I lunge at the change of subject like a life raft. 'You mean Gina?'

'She's the one helping clear your name, yeah?'

I nod. 'I'll tell her I forgot. She'll be okay with it. I'll just have to double my efforts. Not miss any more stake-outs.'

'Do you think she'll find out what happened?'

'I don't think she'll actually solve any mysteries. I guess I'm just playing along. It's kind of fun.'

'Do you *want* to find out what happened?'

'I thought I did, but now it seems like one of those things that just happen. Dogs die for heaps of reasons. I don't think proving I wasn't responsible will change anything. I can't imagine my boss giving me back my old run. Besides, I've been on the new run for a couple of days now, and it's not so bad. I kind of like it. I'm getting used to the hills.'

'Was the chicken raw or cooked?'

'Raw. I'd just buy it at the supermarket and keep it in the fridge.'

'You do know that raw chicken can cause salmonella poisoning, don't you?'

'Whoops.' I had no idea that that could happen. Maybe I *did* kill Satan. It's unlikely, though. I doubt anything the size of a microbe could've taken out that beast. Although it was the common cold that killed the Martians in *War of the Worlds*. Still, Satan was tougher than any old tripod-driving Martian.

From the front of the house comes the sound of a key turning in the lock, then a tall red-headed guy walks in.

'Garth, this is Steven. Steven, this is my housemate, Garth.'

Garth steps forward and offers his hand. I shake it. His grip is firm. I grip firmly back, instinctively playing the two-guys-sizing-each-other-up game. I catch myself doing it and relax a bit.

'Nice to meet you,' I say, trying to make it sound as informal as possible.

'Hi,' says Garth, looking at me, and then at Emma. 'I can see I'm interrupting, so I'll take myself off to bed, then.'

Emma stands up. 'No, don't bother,' she says. 'We can do that instead.' She takes my hand and leads me into her bedroom.

MONDAY

The next morning I'm struggling up the Clarke Street hill. The only thing that keeps me moving forward is the tingling body-memory of last night. I seriously think I'm moving beyond crush with this woman. That's not me, that Steven-shaped figure cycling slowly from house to house, stuffing envelopes into mail-slots, not really. My physical form might be going through the motions of being a postie, but my mind and spirit are still in Emma's bedroom last night, and I'm more than content to leave them there.

We'd talked a while longer in an aimless way, our arms finding comfortable places to rest on each other's bodies. She'd told me about a couple of ideas for poems she'd been working on: one about a bowerbird who builds himself a rocket so that he can break off a piece of the evening sky for his bower; the other about a time when the magpies stop singing the day into being, and people have to construct artificial sunlight and walk about in a perpetual twilight haze. 'I knew you had an interesting mind,' I told her last night, quoting her poem back at her. She rolled her eyes and laughed at the reference.

Even if everything between us, as short-lived as it's been, ended tomorrow I'd still feel lucky for the time we've shared.

'I know it's been a while between drinks, but do you have to be so fuckin' mushy about it?' Wayne's reaction wasn't particularly sympathetic.

'Don't care what you say, Wayne, I'm too happy to take shit from you,' I replied, grinning inanely from lack of sleep and nascent love, as I stuffed my bags with mail.

Wayne laughed and kept on with his own packing. 'So, it's working out all right then, hey?'

I nodded. He slapped me on the back. I shrugged him off and concentrated on unblurring the addresses on the envelopes in front of me.

'Just stick to the comics and leave the poetry to me. "Lucky for the time we've shared." Christ on a crutch.'

'Woman is the mother of the human race; our companion, counsellor and comforter in the pilgrimage of life; or our tempter, scourge and destroyer. Our sweetest cup of earthly happiness, or our bitterest draught of sorrow, is mixed and administered by her hand. She not only renders smooth or rough our path to the grave, but helps or hinders our progress to immortality. In heaven we shall bless God for her aid in assisting us to reach that blissful state, or amidst the torments of unutterable woe in another region we shall deplore the fatality of her influence.'

Wayne and I looked around to see Sully standing behind us, his usual implacable expression smack-bang in the middle of his face.

'How long you been standing there, Sul?' asked Wayne.

'A while.'

'What the hell was that you just said?'

'Something my grandfather used to say.'

'Yeah? A priest, was he?' asked Wayne.

Sully shook his head. 'Just a very devout man.'

'It's a bit full-on, though, don't you think?' I asked.

Sully nodded, and wandered off to his rack. Wayne gave me a look that I'm sure I was returning. We both said nothing and got back to packing.

'Unutterable woe in the nether regions? I knew a guy who had that once,' said Wayne. 'Apparently there's this cream that clears it right up.'

'So, which would you rather have, Wayne? A companion and comforter or a tempter and destroyer?'

'Can't we mix and match it a bit? A companion and a tempter?'

'I don't see why not.' I tried to work out which combination I'd prefer— Emma's definitely a tempter, no question about that, and I suppose she's a companion, too. If I had to choose between comfort and destruction, though, I'd definitely use the first one. Destruction doesn't seem to be on the menu at the moment, which is odd, really, considering my record with relationships.

I cross High Street and start the descent towards Merri Station. Wayne wasn't too far from the mark. It could be fun to get these observations about crushes and stuff down on paper. Not poetry, though. Maybe I'll introduce a girlfriend to the Godlings. Maybe Shiva can have a new love-object. Who would be good for that? Someone from Hindu mythology, probably. I stop at Number 113 and drop an Express Post bag into their slot. Kali, maybe? No, too aggressive. What about Durga? Yeah, maybe. Number 109's got a big bundle today, so has 107. Durga's a bit more tranquil than Kali, but still strong and frightening in her own way. A tempter and a destroyer. I'll have to do some character sketches tonight to see if I can pull it off, but yeah, Durga. I like it. Riding astride a tiger, each of her ten arms bristling with an even more deadly weapon, but her face poised in an inscrutably attractive Mona Lisa smile. I like it.

The sex last night was different again. We're more familiar with each other's bodies, but there's still a lot to learn. It was even more lucid than the last time. We talked to each other in the process. Emma let me know what she wanted me to do for her, and I did my best to oblige. I felt almost overwhelmed by the pleasure of simply touching her, the feel of her skin. It wasn't panic, though. And there was no sense of being smothered or anything. Usually by this stage things have turned up that piss me off, but I haven't noticed a single irritating thing about Emma. I'm more worried that it's the other way around. She doesn't seem to be into the same things as me. She wasn't particularly interested in the search for the Heavy Product Guy.

'Do you really want to know who does it?' she had asked. 'It'll turn out to be some design student with a bunch of stickers. Lots of people do it: This is a Heavy Product, Nat and Ali say We Woz Robbed, the Laughing Robot, Shut up and Shop, the Gorilla stencils in North Fitzroy. Everybody's trying to be the next Andre the Giant. Part of their appeal is that they turn up mysteriously in unexpected places, isn't it? If you find out who it is, you spoil the mystery.'

I had tried to explain the importance of having a quest, but she wasn't convinced.

'What would be more fun, if you ask me, would be to start doing your *own* stickers or stencils. Those comics of yours would make good stickers, especially the monkey with the flaming tail.'

I filed the idea away for future reference. Godlings stickers sounded like a good way to publicise the comic, if I ever got around to finishing it.

The Heavy Product hunt was my and Gina's quest, anyway. Emma had a point about stripping the mystery from the stickers, but I still thought the search was a fun idea. In the back of my mind I think I hoped that if we unmasked the Heavy Product Guy, he might initiate us into his cabal of secret sticker-stickers and we would travel Melbourne end to end, helping him achieve his dream of one sticker for every flat surface in town.

Her taste is still in my mouth, fading with the dawn, but undeniably present. She fell asleep before me and I watched her eyes flutter as my own breathing slowed, and then I slept beside her.

I sigh as I realise I've missed the last four houses, cruising down the hill on autopilot. I turn my bike around, ride back up to Number 28 and then slowly, brakes almost on full, ride back down, stuffing messages from the outside world into all the expectant mailboxes on the street.

There's something for Number 43 Clarke Street today, the first thing I've delivered there in a couple of weeks. It's not impossible for a house to get no mail for two weeks, but it is unusual. Even more interesting, the something is a postcard. It's one of those promotional postcards you get in cafes—the ones that pretend they're not really ads because they look arty and sit on a stylish rack. This one has a picture of a landscape at sunset, all green hills and orange clouds, with the words 'Breaking the Waves' running along the bottom edge. It's pretty. I flip it over and begin to read.

Dear Marvella.
This is awkward, for both of us, and I apoligise for that. I'm going to be in town next month and I wondered if it might be okay to come by and

visit. There's a lot I'd like to talk to you about. If you're okay with that you can write to me at the above address, or if you want you can just call me on (07) 9872 4434.
Tom

It looks like this 'Tom' has had a fight with this 'Marvella', and is trying to patch things up. I wonder what they fought about? Maybe I'm being picky, but if I was Marvella I'd think twice about calling a guy who wanted to apologise but couldn't spell 'apologise'.

'Hey!'

I look up. Standing in the doorway of the house is perhaps the largest woman I've ever seen, wrapped in a dark-red terry-towelling dressing-gown. This must be Marvella. She's wider than the doorway and almost as tall. Shit. Busted reading a customer's mail. Bad form and definitely a disciplinary offence, if reported. Especially considering my recent employment history. I slip the card into the mailbox and make what I hope looks like an apologetic face. Marvella turns sideways and gingerly lowers herself down the two steps onto the path. She walks towards me, breathing heavily with the effort. It's excruciating to watch someone working so hard in order to move so slowly. She looks at me as she advances.

Her words come out in breathy bursts.

'You're not. Supposed to. Read. People's mail. You're just. Supposed to. Deliver it.'

I try for a regretful face. 'Sorry, I was just checking the address was right.' A crap lie, but maybe it'll do the job.

She creeps slowly forward. 'I saw you. Through. The window. You were. Reading it.'

She has every right to be mad. It's awkward, waiting for her to reach the front gate, but I can't bring myself to push off. Instead I watch her close the distance. I pull the card out of the mailbox and hold it out in an attempt to make nice. *Here, I read your private correspondence, but now I'm handing it to you in person to prove what a nice guy I am after all.*

Marvella snatches the card, frowning at me before stuffing it into the pocket of her dressing-gown. She lets out a deep breath and stands before me. I can smell coconutty perfume on her.

'You're not supposed to read people's mail.'

'Umm. Sorry.' I can't meet her gaze. I'm totally in small-dog mode. It's all I can do to stop myself from dropping onto my back and showing her my belly. Bad postie. Bad, *bad* postie. If she reports this, I am so fucked. Fortunately, she seems satisfied with having stared me down. I watch her puff her way back to the house, her ugg boots scuffing on the concrete path. It takes almost two minutes before she's at the steps again. She clambers up onto the veranda, then throws another frown over her shoulder before slamming the door. I picture her reading the card as she waddles back to the breakfast table, gloating with pride over the way she just slapped me down. Maybe she slapped Tom down the same way. Maybe that's why he ran off to Brisbane and now sends her obsequious badly-spelled postcards.

I am in so much deep shit if she reports this. If she reports this, Dave is going to go ballistic. If she reports this, he'll probably move me again—to outer Frankston or something. I sigh, hoping that making me cringe was enough for Marvella.

I hang a left at High Street and coast to the bottom of Rucker's Hill, then hang a right. I cut through the back streets of Northcote, following Aki's suggestions for avoiding as many hills as possible on this run. The only really unavoidable hill is Clarke Street—Marvella's street. But even though it's a bitch to ride up one side, you do at least get the joy of rolling down the other. I've got to be philosophical about these things. The easy-to-cycle flats of my Fitzroy run had made me complacent. Now I'm going to have to work harder to get my job done, and in the process achieve new levels of fitness. Yes, change is a good thing. I think it was the Buddha who said that change is an indication that life is present. If he didn't, I'm sure he meant to.

At Number 16 Charles Street I spy a white cat lounging on the stone wall bordering the front garden. I stop in order to introduce myself properly. I don't have anything for her owners today, but that's no reason to snub this beauty. She arches her back and walks along the wall. I give her a good skritch between the ears. She starts purring. I look down at her and smile.

'Sorry, baby, no crunchies for you. The big bad boss-man wouldn't approve.' It's a shame, really. As if a handful of dry crunchies for a spunky pusscat could ever be a bad thing. Dave's just being an arsehole by making me stop carrying crunchies. But he's the arsehole I work for. I guess I knew that my cat-befriending activities would come under fire in the long run.

I pinch the cat's ear gently and get back on the pedals. Two houses from the corner, the little terrier I've nicknamed Satan Junior is waiting for me in the front yard. She bounds along the fence line and looks up at me as she *yap-yap-yap-yaps* her challenge. 'No chicken for you,' I murmur as I pass. No chicken for anyone any more. The other night I cooked up the three fillets that were left for dinner. Did them with a nice plum sauce and steamed broccoli. It felt weird to be eating Satan's leftovers, but it seemed a waste to throw them out. I'm glad I bought chicken instead of sausages or mince. That dinner was vastly superior to anything I could have done with a handful of cheap sausages.

I finally make it back to the shed and dump my bags. The lack of sleep is catching up with me. I slowly pedal home, feeling the hills of my new run still vibrating in my legs. I wheel my bike out the back and then stagger to my bedroom and collapse, fully-clothed, on my bed, I kick off my boots and slide under the bedclothes.

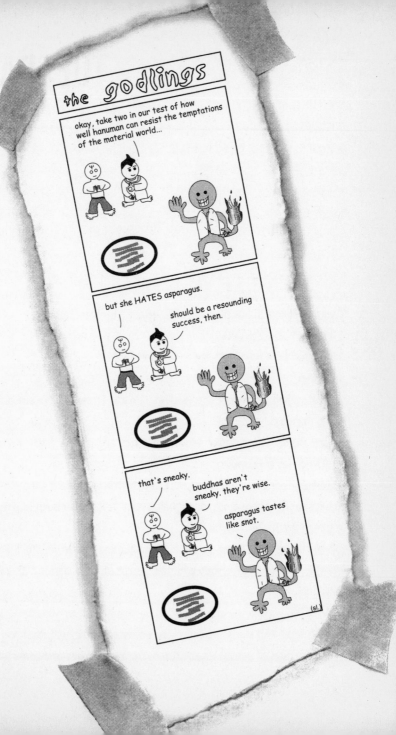

TUESDAY

'Two complaints in less than a week, Steven. This is serious.'

'I know.'

'I'm afraid I'm going to have to respond to this.'

'I know.'

'I was willing to overlook the incident with Mrs Fraser, but I'm afraid this forces my hand.'

I say nothing. Overlook? Moving my run and taking away my cat crunchies was overlooking?

Dave sighs deeply, pretending not to enjoy this. I just want it to be over. If I have to stand here much longer being contrite I'll either burst into tears or punch the fucker. Maybe both.

'I think the best thing to do in this situation is for you to take a few days off to think about whether you're able to perform this job adequately.'

'What?'

David sighs and starts speaking very slowly and quietly. 'I want you to take three days of annual leave, Steven, from tomorrow, and come back to work on Monday with a different attitude. I'll have Sully fill in for you for the rest of the week.'

Making me take leave? Can he do that? I clench my fists behind my back and try to ignore the pins and needles in my chest. 'But I was going to take them at the end of the year. I had plans for that leave.'

David picks up a sheet of paper from his desk. 'According to this you'll still have four days annual leave left. I don't see the problem.'

'But . . .'

'It's either that or I initiate more drastic measures, Steven.' Dave looks levelly at me from his side of the desk. I wait for a moment, trying to match his stare, but I can't. I know I'm in the wrong here. I can't really argue my case.

I click the door shut behind me and walk back to my bike. I concentrate on breathing as calmly as possible. Wayne comes over.

'How was it?'

'I don't think I can talk about it right now. I've got to go.'

'Shit.'

'Yeah. Shit. I'll call you later.'

'Okay.'

On the way home, I almost ride through a red light, but the angry bleating of the car's horn snaps me out of it in time to apply the brakes. As soon as I get in, I'm on the phone.

'Gina? It's me.'

'Well, hello there. What do you want?'

'Um, well, I was kind of ringing to say sorry for the weekend . . .'

'Uh-huh . . .'

'. . . And to see if you want to go out on another stake-out this week.'

'Oh, so you *want* to come along now?'

I pause. I knew this was going to be hard. 'Yeah, look, sorry—I was asleep and hung-over on Saturday and then Sunday I was out with a friend and forgot all about it. Sorry.'

She doesn't reply. I keep my mouth shut.

'I can't do it on my own, Steven. I don't *want* to do it on my own.'

'I know. I'm up for it. I want to help out.'

'Okay, fine. Just don't do it again. I had to cancel a date on Saturday night.'

'With who?'

'Chan.'

'Do I know Chan?'

'I don't think so. I met him at a party.'

'Is he nice?'

'Well, he's spunky. And tall. Yeah, he's nice. He has a nice laugh.'

With apologies and admonitions out of the way we relax and swap stories about the current state of our love lives. Gina's is all over the place, as usual, and I have a bit of a rave to her about Emma, before telling her about today at work.

'Here's what I'm hoping, see—if we can prove I had nothing to do with Satan, then maybe I can at least get my leave back.'

'Like a reward, you mean?'

'Yeah, maybe. You know, proving that I'm a conscientious worker and all that. I dunno. I just need to do something positive, something active. Besides, I've got all this spare time now.'

'Okay, why don't you come over tomorrow and I'll bring you up to speed. Then we can go check out Mr Black Dogs Pouncing.'

'Rae Street?'

'Yeah. None of the other leads have really panned out, so I thought he might be a good next step.'

'You're the boss.'

'Nice of you to say so.'

'Hello, Emma? It's Steven.'

'Oh, hi. How are you?'

'I've been better. Bad day at work. Got busted reading someone's mail. I'm on leave for the rest of the week. It was just a postcard, but my boss didn't see it that way.'

'Oh no. How are you feeling?'

'I'm okay, I think. A bit pissed off with myself . . . I shouldn't have been reading the card, but Dave didn't need to be so shitty about it and . . . Anyway, I was wondering if you were up to anything this week.'

'Yeah, kind of. What were you thinking?'

'I dunno—dinner or something? What are you doing tonight?'

'Busy. How about tomorrow?'

'Ah—no, I've got a stake-out.'

'With Gina?'

'Yeah, with Gina. I'm not staking out with anyone else. This is the only investigation I'm currently involved with.'

'What about the Heavy Product Guy?'

'He's not coming . . . Oh. You know, I never thought about staking him out before. That's a pretty good idea, though . . . What about Thursday?'

'Drinks.'

'Friday?'

'I've got a party in Brunswick, but why don't you come along and meet me there?'

'Um . . . okay. That sounds good. Where's the party?' I scribble down the address. Brunswick. I don't know much about Brunswick. Could be educational.

'Okay, then. See you there.'

'Seeya.' She hangs up.

That was a bit weird. Was she being weird? Is she cooling off on me? Have I done something wrong? Was it something I said? Something I did? Something I did in bed? Oh, god. Stupid crush nerves. I don't know how I feel about not seeing her until Friday. We had sex twice last week, so according to all known relationship algorithms, if things are going well we should have sex at least three times this week, and I don't know if waiting until Friday gives us enough time. Especially if there's something I need to make up for from the last time. I try to think of something I did that she might not have liked, but I can't think of anything, unless it's *everything*. Maybe she thinks I'm a crap shag and she only had sex with me again to confirm her suspicions. I'm not that bad in bed, am I? Maybe I should call some old girlfriends and see what they say. Except I don't think I've kept any of their phone numbers or anything. I suppose I could get them from directory assistance . . .

The phone rings. Emma's calling back. She's changed her mind. I pick it up quickly and jam it against my head, hurting my ear in the process.

'Steven?' It's not Emma. I stifle a groan.

'Hi, Wayne.'

'Don't sound so fucking happy to see me, mate.'

'Sorry, I thought you were Emma.'

'Things going okay?'

'Yeah. No. I have no fucking idea.'

'My advice is don't waste too much time thinking about what women are thinking, mate. Just get on with it when it's there to get on with.'

It's not the best advice I've ever heard, but Wayne's trying to be supportive, and I appreciate that he made the effort.

'So how'd it go at work?'

'Oh, you know. Pretty fucked.'

'Yeah, I heard from Sully. That's fucked, mate.'

'I just can't believe the fucker would force me to take leave. I didn't know he could do that.'

'Maybe you want to talk to the union about this, or something.'

'I dunno. I don't want to make any more trouble . . .'

'Look, I'm heading up to the Nape for a beer. Come on down. Drown your sorrows.'

'I tell you, I didn't know if I was going to cry or punch the fucker.'

'Come on. I'll drop in and pick you up on the way.'

'Yeah, okay.'

At 2 a.m. I stagger through the front door, drop my keys in the hallway, flop onto the couch, nod off for a minute, then lurch upright and head into my bedroom. I tear down the scrap of paper with Emma's phone number and carry it into the hallway. I pick up the phone and unsteadily dial the sequence of numbers that floats before me.

'Hi. You've called Emma, Garth, Celine and Biggy. Leave a Message.'

Shit. A message. I don't think I'm in the right shape to leave one of those. I hang up, then think of something to say and pick the handset up again. Bugger. They hung up. I go to dial the number again, then forget what I was going to say. I stand still for a moment, hoping that it'll come back to me, but my mind is a beer-soaked blank. I stumble into my room for a pen and some paper to write it down when I do remember.

the godlings

okay, if you're such an enlightened individual, what number am i thinking of?

eleven.

wow, that's right.

and you're wearing red underpants.

and your mother's going to call you tonight to complain that you never call.

spooky.

(sl.)

WEDNESDAY

Daytime stake-outs aren't any more interesting than evening stake-outs, but I'm on my best behaviour today despite my massive hangover. We're parked opposite the weirdo's house, two hours into today's proceedings. Gina has her notebook open at the middle page, and is jotting down some stuff. I peer over her shoulder.

'You've been busy.'

'Mmmm.'

'Hey, did I tell you what Emma said about the Heavy Product sticker guy?'

'Yeah, you did.'

'Oh. Did I tell you about that poem she's going to write about the bowerbird?'

Gina looks up at me, her pen tucked in the corner of her mouth. 'Yeah. You did.'

'Why are you looking at me like that?'

'You've got some massive crush on this girl, haven't you?'

I blush.

'I'm not hanging shit on you, Steven. I just can't remember the last time you went gaga over a girl. You're usually so . . . aloof.'

'Aloof?'

'Yeah. Not really interested. Kind of like you're playing along.'

'Well . . . she's different from the others.'

'How?'

'She's older.' I take another sip of V, feeling the nasty sugary taste coat my tongue, but tolerating it for the sake of today's hangover. I slump in my seat and look across the road. Nothing's happening. 'Maybe he's out.'

'Sharon was older.'

'Only by a year.'

'So how old is she?'

'Umm . . . twenty-seven. And she's smarter.'

Gina whistles. 'I went out with a twenty-seven year old guy once, but I think it's different for guys. They don't smarten up for ages.'

'I should probably say something to defend my gender, but I can't think of anything.'

'Rest my case.' She leans forward and squints at me. 'You've got something on your face, there,' she says, motioning to my forehead.

I turn the rear vision mirror around and take a look. There's a faint black smudge above my right eyebrow. 'Oh, yeah,' I say. 'I fell asleep on a texta last night.'

Gina nods as though it's the most sensible answer she's ever heard and resumes scribbling in her casebook. I turn the mirror back the way it was, then take a big swig of V. A pale-blue Datsun turns into the street and drives past us.

'Look,' says Gina.

Goatee Guy is coming out of the front door at Number 43. He walks past us, carrying a dark-green backpack on one shoulder.

'Come on,' says Gina, opening her door.

'Where?'

'We're going to check out his place.'

'What?' She doesn't hear me. She's opening the boot. She pulls out a shovel. Hung-over as I am, I jump quickly out of the car. Too quickly. I trip on the gutter and only just manage to avoid falling. 'What are you going to do with that?'

She looks at the shovel as if it's the first time she's noticed it. 'This?'

'Yeah, that.'

'It's just in case we find anything.'

I keep my mouth shut. I follow her across the road to the cobblestoned lane a few doors up. We scuttle to the cross-lane, past abandoned washing machines and graffiti distorted by the corrugations of back fences. Gina turns the corner.

'Okay, 53, 51, 49 . . . Here we are. Rear entrance, 43 Rae Street.' Gina rattles the gate. It's locked. 'Gimme a boost,' she says, and throws the shovel over the fence.

I watch it arc and hear the muffled thump of what I hope is just a shovel hitting dirt. I shrug, and bend down, linking my fingers for Gina to step up. 'Fuck, you're heavy,' I say as her Doc Martens grind into my palm.

'Shoosh.' She pulls herself up onto the wall, swivels into a sitting position and drops out of sight. A second later the gate opens.

'Come on.'

I follow her in. The backyard has a patch of lawn, a vegie garden and a Hills Hoist at the end of a little concrete path that leads to the back step of the house. Against the back fence is a small shed.

'You keep a lookout,' she says, and ducks inside the shed.

I'm starting to feel really seedy. I should have drunk more water before collapsing into bed last night. I wish I'd brought the other can of V I had stashed in Gina's car. I look nervously around the yard, keeping one eye on the back door. I can hear Gina rummaging around, shuffling things on shelves and banging things together as she moves them. A lone white sock hangs from the Hills Hoist, attached by a bright-yellow peg. Gina keeps making investigatory noises. A sparrow hops around the vegie patch. I watch it hop. This isn't so bad. I'm comfortable with this kind of low-impact proactivity.

The back door opens. Goatee Guy steps into the back yard. I let out a little yelp.

'What are you *doing*?' screams Goatee Guy.

Gina comes out of the shed. 'Oh fuck,' she says.

Goatee Guy goes back inside.

'I think we should get out of here,' says Gina. I nod.

We scoot through the gate, leaving it to bang against the fence as we pound up the lane and into Rae Street. We race across the road. Gina fumbles with her keys, gets in, unlocks my door. She turns the key in the ignition. Goatee Guy is coming out of the lane. He's holding a cricket bat.

'Can we just go now?' I whine. This is not fun. Definitely not fun. Goatee Guy sprints across the road just as the engine turns over. Gina puts it into gear, but Goatee Guy is already next to us. He raises the cricket bat and brings it down on the bonnet. It makes a god almighty crash. I try to push myself backwards through the seat.

'*Fuck!*' screams Gina, putting the car in reverse. Too fast. The gears grind.

'*Who sent you?*' screams Goatee Guy, staring through the windscreen with livid eyes.

For a moment I consider getting out of the car and saying, 'Hey, chill out, guy, it's me—Natasha', but instead I lock my door and yell at Gina. It seems safer.

'Can we get the *fuck out of here?*' I scream.

Gina backs out and Goatee Guy steps into the road and swings the bat above his head.

'*You tell Di Stasio to stay away from me!*'

On 'away' he lunges forward and swings the bat down, crashing into the bonnet again. We lurch forward. Goatee Guy jumps out of the way and we take off. He stays in the middle of the road, brandishing the bat.

'Fuck fuck *fuck.*' says Gina.

I sit forward and stare into space, listening to the sound of my heartbeat. 'That was a little bit intense,' I mumble.

'No kidding,' says Gina.

Neither of us says another word until we pull up outside Gina's place in North Carlton. She turns off the engine and we both sit quietly for a moment.

'Cup of tea?' asks Gina.

I nod and unbuckle my seatbelt. I don't even remember putting it on.

'I don't see what's so funny.'

Gina is sprawled over the kitchen table, pissing herself laughing. I'm trying to stop shaking. Two cups of tea sit on the table between us.

'Sorry,' she says, sitting back and pushing her hair out of her eyes. 'Wooh, what a rush.'

'Yeah, if you're into being threatened with violence by total lunatics.'

She takes a sip of her tea. 'My poor, poor car,' she says, shaking her head. 'Shit.' She sits up straight.

'What?'

'I left the shovel there. Damn.'

'We had other things on our mind.'

'Maybe I should go back for it.'

'What?'

'Kidding.'

I sigh and drink my tea.

Gina gets up and rummages in the fridge. 'But think of it,' she says. 'Our very own chase scene. How cool?'

'Whatever.'

She plonks a couple of dip containers and a block of cheese on the table. 'Anyway, I didn't find anything in the shed. Nothing that makes me think he's our man, anyway. He's too far from Best Street, besides. I reckon it's back to Ma Fraser's place tomorrow. Check out around the back. Do some more lanework.'

I dip some cheese in the hommus and chew quietly.

'Steven? You okay?'

I keep chewing. 'Steven?'

I break off another piece of cheese.

'Steven?' Gina nudges my elbow.

'No, I'm not okay,' I say, looking her straight in the eye. 'That was really fucking scary and really fucking stupid, Gina.'

She looks back at me without saying anything. I go on. 'I'm just . . . I don't think I want to play this game any more. It's getting out of hand.'

'Game? You think this is a game?'

I stare at her.

'I'm not doing this purely for my enjoyment, Steven. I'm doing this to help you out, and if you aren't interested in helping me help you . . .'

'Bullshit, Gina,' I say.

She shuts her mouth with a snap. Her eyes narrow.

I dunk the cheese in the hommus again, stalling for time to figure out where to go with this. 'Bullshit,' I repeat, trying to soften my tone before I continue. 'You're totally doing this for your enjoyment. It's all part of your thing with Jessica Fletcher. You're doing this so that you can pretend to be the lady detective who's always right about things. Maybe there's a zine article in it for you, too.'

'I'm trying to help you get your job back,' she hisses at me. 'I'm trying to clear your name.'

'I haven't lost my job. And you can't clear my name. There's nothing to clear. What—you think that hanging out in parked cars watching nothing happen is detective work? You think breaking into someone's shed is an investigation? It's not, Gina. It's play-acting. You're not going to find out anything this way, because there's nothing to find out! The dog's dead, I didn't do it, and nobody really cares either way! We're not living in a fictional universe where everything's a clue and it all ties up neatly at the end, you know. This is the Real World, not some crazy comedic detective story for teenagers. You should keep that in mind.'

'It's not play-acting,' Gina says.

'It is,' I insist. 'And it's boring play-acting, too. I'm not getting off on any of this—you are. I've got a life outside this stupid detective fantasy.'

'*What* life?' Gina yells. 'Your crappy job that gives you nothing but grief? Your new girlfriend, who's too busy to see you and who you'll probably dump in a week? Steven, what do you do when you're not hanging out with me? If it wasn't for me you'd just be sitting at home, fucking around on the Internet! Jesus, I put up with your whiny sidekick routine enough, but this is fucking priceless.'

'Is that how you see me? I'm your *sidekick*?'

'Now you've got this older, smart woman to hang out with you can't be bothered spending time with me any more, right?'

'What, are you jealous?' I regret the words as soon as they leave my mouth.

Gina pushes her chair back from the table, then calmly gets up to put her cup in the sink. 'If that's what you think,' she says in a level tone that makes my stomach clench, 'if you can't see that this has *nothing* to do with wherever you're sticking your dick, if you can't understand that this is just about helping me out when I ask for your help . . . If you can't see that I've been doing this as much for you as *anyone* else, then you can just fuck off.'

I feel like she's slapped me in the face. My immediate impulse is to slap her back, but instead I stand up and walk down the hallway. 'Fine,' I say.

The door slams shut behind me.

the godlings

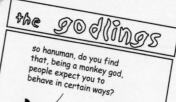

so hanuman, do you find that, being a monkey god, people expect you to behave in certain ways?

oh, hell yeah. that whole 'mischievous' schtick dogs me wherever i go. if anything goes wrong, i'm usually the first to get the blame. plus, people are always offering me bananas. it gets kind of rough.

and your tail is on fire.

..and my tail is on fire.

do either of you know anything about my bedroom burning down?

(sl.)

THURSDAY

I wake up at four-thirty, like I always do. I look over at the alarm clock and wonder why it hasn't gone off. Then I remember I don't have to work today, and roll over to try to get back to sleep. I replay yesterday's events in my mind: the chase, the argument. I shouldn't have been so mean to Gina, but I wasn't thinking. I was scared and pissed off and hung-over, and now I don't know if I can apologise. I don't know if I want to. Does Gina really think that all I do is tag along after her and complain? Is that what I've been doing? Maybe she's got a point. The guerrilla editing was her idea, and she was the one who started the hunt for the Heavy Product Guy. She makes her own zines. What do I do? Hell, *everybody I know* makes their own something: Wayne and Emma have their poetry books, Gina has *Zines, She Wrote*, Van has the magazine . . . what do I have? A bunch of comic strips that sit on my hard drive and do nothing.

I bury my head in the pillow. Maybe it's time to change the way I do things. I've been arsing about with the idea of putting out a Godlings comic for a week now, and I'm no closer to finishing it. I should take Emma's suggestion seriously, too—make some stickers and put them up around the place. Fuck it, that's what I'll do today. I'll get active. I'll make positive changes in my life. I'll show everyone that I'm not just a follower, not just a sidekick. I'll show them that I'm an empowered creative individual in my own right. And once I've taken over the world using comics and stickers, then I'll get started on eliminating Third World poverty.

I roll over and look at the clock. Eleven-thirty. Shit. Half the day's gone and I haven't done anything with it. I get out of bed, have a quick shower, then boot up my computer and shuffle through the Godlings printouts that are still on my desk. I open the notepad program and type a list.

TO DO!!!

1. *Finish strips*
2. *Photocopy*
3. *Stapling?*
4. *Stickers?*
5. *Put comics in shops (ask Wayne)*

I add 'Make list' above number one, then re-number the other points. That way I can cross it off as soon as I print the list out, and feel like I've accomplished something already. I leave a message on Wayne's answering machine to call me when he gets home. In the meantime I think I'll take advantage of the proactive new me and clean my room.

I sit in my room, all books back on the shelf, all CDs packed away, piles of important papers neatly stacked on the end of the desk. I'm playing with the layout of the comic, working out how to squeeze two strips onto a page to make it more like a booklet and less like a sheaf of pages stapled together. I've pulled apart a couple of Gina's zines to see how she did it. If I set the pages to landscape layout and re-orient the strips, I can photocopy them double-sided and get four strips on each page. There's a knock at the door just as I'm tweaking the final page. It's Wayne.

'Hey. How you doing?'

I shrug. 'Okay. How's work?'

'Fine. You're not missing anything.'

We head to the kitchen and I make coffee. Wayne reaches into his backpack, pulls out a long black stapler and sets it on the table. I let out a low whistle of appreciation.

'Meet Staplor,' says Wayne. 'He's my sidekick.'

I wince. 'Thanks for bringing him over.'

'No problem. You sure you don't want me to come with you to Officeworks?'

'Nah, it's fine. I think I'll manage with what you told me on the phone.'

'It's pretty much just trial and error, anyway.'

I plonk the coffee in front of him and sip at my own. Staplor is heavy. I hold him like a baseball bat, or a sword. 'He's pretty cool.'

'Best stationery purchase ever.'

'So, did you bring the list?'

He pulls a crumpled piece of paper out of his pocket and flips it over the table. 'There's about five places you definitely want to go to, and they're all pretty close. Two in the city, one in Fitzroy . . .'

'That's Polyester, yeah?'

'Yeah. Zine central, pretty much. But Sticky, the new place in the city under Flinders Station, is really good too. If you only do two, do those two.'

'Wanna see it?'

I show him what I've printed so far.

'I like the cover.'

'I was thinking of doing them colour.'

'Expensive . . .'

'Yeah, but what the fuck, right? If you're going to do it, do it right, right?'

'Isn't that a song?'

'Is it? I don't know.'

He hands the pages back to me. 'I get a free copy, right?'

'Fuck you.'

'Excellent.' He looks at his watch. 'Well, I better go. I'm catching up with Trudy.'

I raise my eyebrows.

'Yeah, shut up,' he says. 'How's things with Emma?'

'Dunno. I'm seeing her tomorrow night at someone's party in Brunswick.'

'So she hasn't dumped you yet.'

'Fuck you, Wayne.'

'I better go.' He hands me a box of staples. 'Take care of Staplor.'

I accept the box reverently, and bow my head with respect.

Later that night I'm sitting in front of the TV with sixty collated and stapled newly-minted first-run copies of *Godlings,* Issue 1. The colour cover has come out better than I hoped—as it should have, at a dollar a page. I spent more money than I'd expected, mainly on buggering up the double-sided copying, but eventually I got it happening. I even found some sticker paper that can be run through a photocopier, so tonight I'm going to design promotional stickers that I'll run through the colour copier at Officeworks tomorrow before heading out to put this sucker in the shops.

I stack the comics into piles of five and slip rubber bands around them from the stash I liberated from work a while ago. I arrange them on my desk, next to the computer, with my new receipt and invoice book, then boot up and start working on phase two of Operation Sidekick No More.

the **godlings**

i can't believe my whole room burned down... everything i had was in there.

i lost my CDs, my books, my godzilla toys...

don't worry about it, shiva. after all, it's not the material possessions we accumulate in this life that are important. it's the things we learn that make us who we are.

so what am i supposed to have learned from this?

never let a monkey-god with a flaming tail sleep over.

(sl.)

FRIDAY

Who would have thought Brunswick was so big? I should have photo-copied the map. I should have done a trial ride out here to get my bearings.

I slow down at another cross street. Nope, that's not it either. I try to think positive. It's good exercise. Which means I'll turn up at the party, where I probably won't know anyone, tired and sweaty. I come to another cross street, which also turns out to be the wrong one. This is just fucked. On the map it was only five blocks up from Lygon Street, but that's the seventh street I've passed and none of them has been O'Dowd. Unless it was the one on the left, without a sign. I don't want to double back yet. Give it three more blocks.

I wish I wasn't on my own tonight, but Wayne was busy, Van wasn't interested and I couldn't bring Gina, though I tried. Her mum took my message and told me she'd pass it on, but, just quietly, she told me Gina was unlikely to come.

'I don't know what you said to her, love, but it certainly got her back up.'

'I know. Things got a little out of hand.'

'So I gather. I think you've got some work cut out for you, sweetheart.'
There was a pause. 'She tells me you have a young lady in your life.'

I nodded, then replied so she could hear me. 'Yeah.'

'That sounds nice,' she enthused. 'I'm sure she's lovely. You should
come over for afternoon tea some time, so we can have a proper gossip.'

I smiled, remembering nights spent with the three of us around a table
of red wine and a bowl or two of warm olives. I wondered if we'd ever
do that again.

'Well, tell Gina I called.'

'I will, love. Take care.'

I couldn't think of anyone else to invite, given that my main plan is to get
absolutely shit-faced as quickly as possible in order to put this crap week
behind me. Nobody else I know would put up with how obnoxious I'll be
after I drink the four Coopers longnecks clinking in the bag slung over my
back. It's better that I go solo tonight, lost in the Brunswick twilight. I'm seriously contemplating just heading home and drinking these beers in my
bedroom while surfing for Internet porn. But at least I'll get to see Emma
tonight. Fucking Brunswick. Who the hell lives in Brunswick, anyway?

I pass another street that isn't O'Dowd. Time to double back. I spin the
bike around, and something explodes behind me. I close my eyes and
swear under my breath. There's no mistaking the crash and splatter of a
full bottle of beer shattering on bitumen.

I look at the pile of brown glass resting in a foaming white puddle just
behind me. Ah. I slip my bag off my shoulder. One of the longnecks has
worked its way through a hole in the bottom of my bag. I count slowly to
ten, looking for the humour in this situation. I can't see it. I sigh deeply,
shake my head and get back on my bike. I don't think Brunswick likes me
very much.

I find O'Dowd Street exactly where it should have been. I turn left and trundle down to Number 44, cradling the bottom of my bag in case any more beer makes a break for freedom. The house is all lit up, with music and laughter drifting out onto the footpath. I take a deep breath, psyching myself up to enter a house full of strangers armed with only three beers and the foulest mood I've been in for a long time.

Someone has tied a sad, deflated balloon to the front gate in proper party fashion. I wander up to the open front door. A bunch of people are sitting around on an old couch, smoking and talking. I nod to them as I pass, and one guy nods back, checking me out to see if he knows me.

It's a big party, and it's in full swing. The lounge room is littered with people in various stages of inebriation. The stereo pumps out bass-heavy dance music, but nobody's dancing. I can see through into the kitchen and out to the backyard, where there's a bonfire.

No sign of Emma.

I find the bathroom and stash my beers among all the other bottles in the bath full of ice.

Talk swirls around me.

'. . . never expected that he would actually go through with it!'

'. . . told him I wasn't his goddamn glory hole!'

'You go, girl!'

'. . . not a lion, that's a giraffe!'

'I really prefer his early, funny stuff.'

'. . . how he got the whole thing in there in the first place!'

I dive into the throng to see if I can find Emma, or at least a conversation I can insinuate myself into.

Later, I'm slugging straight from the bottle and checking out the CDs stacked in the cabinet under the stereo. The only stuff here I recognise is old and boring. James Brown, Stevie Wonder, Prince. There's got to be something here that's worth listening to.

'Find anything?' A shaven-headed woman squats down next to me.

I shake my head. 'Not much,' I say.

She reaches out to flip through the discs. 'What do you mean not much?' she asks, pulling one of the Stevie Wonder CDs out. 'This is a great album.'

I watch her sceptically and take another mouthful of beer as she changes the CD. The people dancing around us nod appreciatively when the first few notes come through the speakers. She looks down at me and smiles with satisfaction, then joins the dancers. I watch her dance for a bit, then keep flipping through the discs. Right at the back I find a copy of Ray Fayne's *Pretty Plastic People*, which I rest beside the stereo for later. I watch the dancers for a while, and scan the room for any familiar faces. I drain the dregs from my bottle. Where the hell is Emma?

Back in the bathroom I grab my second beer, flick the bottle top against the wall of the bathroom and head out to the backyard. It's huge. There's a bonfire set up in an old metal rubbish bin. I listen in on conversations while holding my hands out to the warmth of the flames. They're all about people I don't know. Why don't people talk about more abstract things that anyone could have an opinion on? Who cares if Jenny's still overseas and Mirab broke up with his girlfriend?

'So who here understands the Schrödinger's cat paradox?' I call out to the group around the fire. A couple of them look up at me. I take another slug of beer. Maybe I should have eaten something before I came out. Nobody takes my conversational bait, so I elaborate. 'You know—the cat in the box? It's a quantum physics thing.'

'Don't know, mate,' says a guy in a brown jumper. He gives his friend a look and they resume their conversation.

'Never mind,' I mumble. I stare into the flames for a minute, then head back inside.

A girl with green dreadlocks comes out of the bathroom and I step inside. I crouch in front of the bathtub, and try to find my last beer, but it's not here. Fine. I'll just have to invoke the unspoken rule: he who placeth three bottles in the bath taketh three bottles out. To be fair, I shouldn't steal anything more expensive than the beer I brought. I settle on a stubby of Melbourne. Not my favourite, but not irreplaceable for whoever brought it.

'Hey! That's my beer!' A guy with short black hair and a maroon rollneck jumper is standing over me.

I opt for the truth. 'Sorry about that, but someone's nicked mine.'

'Unspoken rule, hey?' The guy laughs. I hand him his stubby, nodding sheepishly.

'I'm Han,' he says, offering me his un-beer-laden hand.

'Steven Lydon.'

'Any relation to—?'

'Nah.' I shake my head at the expected reference.

'So you're out of booze? I know where there's some vodka, if you're up for it.'

I smile with relief. A friendly person at last. In the kitchen, Han ducks down in front of the sink and opens up the cabinet doors. He reaches inside and pulls out a plastic bottle labelled 'bathroom cleaner'. He winks and pours me a glass. I smell it. It's vodka. I take a mouthful and repress the kickback gag reflex. It's been a while since I drank vodka straight.

'So you live here?' I ask.

'Yeah, me, Ling and Jamie. Who do you know here?'

'I'm supposed to be meeting my friend Emma here, but I don't think she's turned up yet.'

'Emma Monori? Poet Emma? I think she's out the front with Jamie.'

'Steven!'

Emma is sitting wedged between a guy with short blond hair wearing a blue blazer, and a dark-haired woman in purple fishnets and a burgundy dress. I kneel down in front of her.

'Hi,' I say, my head rocking to the side. 'I've been looking for you all night.'

'I just got here,' she says. 'Been here long?'

I take her hand and kiss her lightly on the knuckles. 'I've been here long.' I slurp at the vodka. It's really good to see her. I feel much better now.

'I saw your bike outside,' she says. 'I was just going to come in to find you.'

I beam at her.

'Have you guys met?'

I shake my head. 'Don't know anyone here,' I say, ''cept you.'

Emma gently extricates her hand from mine. 'This is Ling and Jamie. This is Steven.'

'How are things inside?' asks Ling.

'Okay,' I shrug, taking another sip of vodka. The glass is almost empty. I look up at Emma. She looks really pretty tonight. She's wearing a soft blue jumper and blue jeans. Her hair is tied back so I can see her ears. I suppress the urge to lunge forward and bite them.

'I'll go see what's happening out the back,' says Jamie. He rests his hand on Emma's shoulder for a moment that seems longer than it should be.

Emma smiles and looks up at him as he stands. I wait for him to take his hand off her shoulder, then quickly flop down in his place. The softness of the backrest against my head is soothing. I close my eyes.

'You okay?' asks Emma.

'I made a comic,' I say, leaning up against her shoulder. 'I took it to the shops today. Rode all around town. Had a receipt book and everything.'

'Where'd you go?'

'Missing Link, Polyester, a couple of comic shops in the city . . .'

'What did you think of Polyester?'

'They were really nice. Why?'

'I just think they're creepy. All those bongs and porno books. My book never sold very well there, but I guess it's poetry. Not really the right customers.'

'But your stuff's really good.' I lift my head from her shoulder to emphasise my point. I'm too floppy to hold it though, and I sink back down.

'That's sweet.'

This is nice. I could go to sleep right now. I listen to Ling and Emma's conversation, but I don't take much in. Instead, I focus on the soothing vibration of Emma's shoulder as her voice passes through her body. I can feel the tension sluicing out of me. The vodka is warming me from the inside out. The stereo is still playing Stevie Wonder. I recognise the song. It's that superstition one. I suck down the last of the vodka and settle into Emma's shoulder. This is nice.

Emma nudges me upright. 'We're going in to have a dance. Want to come?'

I shake my head. 'No, thanks.' She's going? I just found her after wandering around this horrible party and now she's going?

She stands up. I grab her hand. She frowns. 'Are you okay?'

'It's been a rough week.'

She sits down again.

I lean over and kiss her. She kisses back, and runs her fingers through my hair. I move my mouth onto her neck. She tilts her head back and laughs.

'Let's go home,' I say.

'I just got here.' She pulls back and looks into my face.

'I'm tired,' I say, hooking one finger over the collar of her jumper.

'And I'm not,' she says.

I straighten up. 'Does that mean you don't want to go?'

She nods.

I breathe out noisily. 'Well, great. Fucking great. I ride all the way over to the arse end of the world, smash my beer on the way, then I have to hang around with a bunch of people I don't know who steal my beer and make me listen to crap music, all so I can see you, and when you finally show up you don't want to spend any time with me.'

'Hey,' she says. 'I just got here. I didn't say I don't want to spend time with you. I want to stay here for a while. It's been a shitty week for me, too, you know, not that you've asked or anything. I'd like a chance to unwind a bit and catch up with some people I haven't seen for a while. Just because you want me to take you home doesn't mean I have to, Steven. It's not like we're going out or anything.'

We're not? I fold my arms across my chest. 'Fine,' I say. 'I'll go home then.'

'If that's what you want to do. Look,' she says more gently, 'I didn't mean to snap at you, but you snapped first. I'm just saying I'd like to take things slowly, yeah? We don't have to sleep together every time we see each other, you know.'

I look over at her. 'Whatever.'

She stands up and rests a hand on my shoulder. 'Maybe you should go home,' she says. 'Call me when you're feeling better, hey?' She bends down and pecks me on the cheek. 'See you,' she says, then goes back inside. The stereo is still playing Stevie Wonder.

The wind whips past my ears as I slam each leg down hard, like a piston. I'm not sitting on this bicycle, I'm part of it, the engine part, the motive force. The booze is fuel for my exertions tonight, and in theory these exertions will burn the booze from my system, leaving me clean and sober when I finally arrive home. I pass another party, another group of people crammed into one house to make noise and soak up each other's body heat. Wonder if there's anyone at that party who's made as big a dick of themselves as I just did? It's not enough that I've made my best mate madder at me than she's ever been before, is it? I have to go and act like a spoiled child in front of the woman I'm keen on, too.

I hate apologising. I'm no good at it. I always end up starting another fight. I try to imagine a life without Gina, but I can't. We've never really argued like this before. It's unsettling. I feel off-balance.

'It's not like we're going out or anything.' I can't believe Emma said that. Well, fine. Then we're *not* going out. I'll call her tomorrow and tell her it's over. And who the fuck is Jamie, anyway? But the thought of not kissing Emma any more is like being repeatedly punched in the stomach. If I don't apologise to Gina and I break up with Emma then I'll be all alone, just me and the monkey comics. I should apologise to Emma, shouldn't I? Wait—it's not Emma I should be apologising to, it's Gina. Yeah. I'll call her tomorrow and say sorry. Suck up. Write her a stupid apologetic postcard if I have to, only I'll make sure I spell 'apologise' right. And I'll call Emma too. I don't have a choice here. I either apologise to both of them or I learn to put up with a life without two of the most remarkable people I've ever met. But what if an apology isn't enough? What if I've gone too far? I need to go to bed. I don't think I have the energy to worry like this for much longer. I clear my mind and concentrate on pedalling.

The lights are still on at home. I leave my bike in the hallway and head for the kitchen to grab a bottle of water. Something catches my shin and trips me; something metal. I hiss a curse, then backtrack and turn on the light.

In the middle of the lounge room is a big red circular sign on a pole, with SLOW on one side and STOP on the other. I bend down to get a better look.

And resting on the kitchen table is a giant orange hazard light, dimly flicking on and off. Must be low on batteries. I laugh and pick it up. It's heavy.

Just then, I hear a faint noise coming from the bathroom. There it is again. It sounds like coughing. Maybe it's Van. I open the bathroom door slowly in case she's naked, like last time. Whoever it is coughs again. I flick the light on.

It wasn't coughing. It was quacking. Floating in the bath is a yellow duckling.

'Hello, little fella,' I whisper, and crouch down beside him. He flaps his little wings as I pick him up, but I gently wrap my fingers around him and bring him up to eye level. He's just a baby. 'Where did you come from?' He doesn't answer. 'Have you come to live with us?' He blinks at me and sneezes. 'You'll have to pull your weight around here, you know,' I tell him. 'Kitty is twenty bucks a week, and the dishes roster is up above the sink.'

He gently bites my thumb with his beak.

'Are you cute, or what?' I ask him. He chuckles. I nuzzle his beak with my nose, then set him back in the water. He shakes himself all over, then paddles to the end of the bath. I turn off the light and listen for a moment to the quiet chuckling quacks before heading to my room. At least the duck loves me.

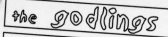

SATURDAY

I wake to the sound of rhythmic thumping in Van's room and remember a conversation we once had about the best hangover cures. I suggested that Vegemite on toast was best, but Van was a strong advocate for orgasms.

I'm not going to get back to sleep, so I shuffle into the kitchen. I switch on the kettle and plonk two slices of bread in the toaster, then grab the Vegemite. I'd prefer an orgasm, really I would, but after last night it's probably toast from here on in.

I slather the toast with black yeasty goodness, dunk a teabag and add milk and three sugars. Five slices later Van walks into the kitchen. She's surprised to see me, and pulls her robe across her chest. I nod good morning, making strict eye contact.

'Thought you wouldn't be home last night,' she says, leaning in the doorway. 'We figured we could be a bit noisy this morning.'

'Have you thought of a name for it yet?'

Van looks up, her hair straggling around her face. 'What?' she rasps, pulling her robe tighter.

'The duck.'

She grins and bites her bottom lip. 'Not yet.'

'Where'd you find it?'

'That's the funny thing. It was just wandering down the street, about a block from here. We thought we'd better take it in before some cat got it.'

'So what are you going to do?'

'Well,' she looks at me to gauge my reaction, 'we could keep him for a while and put up notices around to see if anyone claims him.'

I visualise a telephone pole with a FOUND DUCK notice sticky-taped to it, a hand-drawn picture of the duckling above our phone number.

'How do you know it's a he?'

'I don't,' Van says. 'Are you any good at sexing ducks?'

'I wouldn't know where to look.'

'Underneath.'

I give her a blank stare.

'You grew up with chooks, right?' she asks.

'I just used to chase them around the backyard, and collect their eggs. It was pretty easy to tell the boys from the girls. If it crows, it's a boy.'

I get up to peek in the bathroom. The duckling is curled up on the bathmat. I gently nudge the bathmat into the corner. We don't want to step on our newest housemate.

'You doing anything tomorrow night?'

'No, why?'

'I was thinking of inviting Emma over for dinner.'

'Ooooh,' she sings. 'The new gi-i-rlfriend . . .'

'Would that be okay?'

'Gonna impress her with your cooking, are you?'

'I kind of acted like a dick last night.'

'I presume you mean that in a non-sexual way.'

I don't respond.

'Yeah, that's cool.' Van stands up and stretches, her robe loosening slightly. I look away.

'I think I need a shower,' she says.

'Watch out for the duck.'

I spend most of the day aimlessly wandering around the house. I play with the duck for a while, work on the FOUND DUCK notice, have a go at some Godlings, and try out mental scripts for the phone calls I'm planning to make to Gina and Emma. I end up confusing myself with the various scenarios I play and replay in my mind, so after dinner I decide that the best thing to do is to be honest and apologetic and, if need be, a little bit pathetic.

Gina still isn't answering, which alleviates my nervousness about what I'm going to say, but increases my anxiety about whether I'll ever have an opportunity to say it. I leave a friendly sounding request for her to return my call, and hang up, trying not to feel freaked out.

Emma answers her phone after a couple of rings. I take a deep breath when I hear her voice.

'Feeling any better?' she asks.

'Yeah. Sorry I cracked it,' I say, going for the right tone of voice, using the equation 'quiet plus slow minus whiny equals okay' as a guide.

'That's okay.' She sounds neutral. I think the equation is working.

'Did you have a good time?' I ask.

'After you left, yeah.' I can hear the challenge in her voice. I cop it sweet.

'Ling seems nice,' I offer.

'She is. You should have stuck around.'

'You're right. I'm sorry. I was tired. A bit drunk,' I say, before launching into phase two of the plan. 'I was wondering if you were doing anything tomorrow night?' That sounded a little whiny, but I think I can get away with it.

'Not really.'

'Would you like to come over for dinner? Sort of my way of apologising for last night.' Better. Less whiny.

She pauses. 'Yeah, okay,' she says. I quietly sigh in relief. 'You want me to bring anything?'

'No, I've got it covered. Is Indian okay? Chutneys and pappadams and shit?'

'What time?'

'Seven-thirty?'

'Okay, see you then.'

I hang up. That went okay. I think that went okay.

SUNDAY

Six-thirty Sunday night rolls around and I'm putting the finishing touches to dinner. A pot of oil on the stove is smoking, waiting for the pappadams. Next to it, my cast-iron wok is bubbling with a thick tan sauce, the chickpeas floating on top and the occasional island of cauliflower floret breaking the surface. Sitting on the table are the only two bowls that match each other. Looks okay to me.

Van wanders in, fiddling with an earring. 'What about some candles?'

'You don't think that's too much?'

'It'd be a nice touch,' she suggests. 'I've got some in my room.'

'You sure you don't want to stay? I've made heaps,' I call after her, hoping she'll say no.

'That's okay. Sean and I are going for a drink, but dibs on any leftovers.' She sets two candlesticks on the table. 'How's that?'

I give the curry a stir and check my watch. Twenty to.

'Aw, you're nervous.'

I ignore her and stick my head into the bathroom to see how the duckling is doing. He's asleep again on the bathmat.

'Can I stick him in your room?'

'Sure,' Van says, plonking herself down on the couch. 'Take a load off,' says Van, patting the seat beside her.

I flump down and kick my feet up on the coffee table. I check my watch.

'She'll be here, don't worry,' says Van.

I nod and lean back on the couch.

Sean picks Van up at around seven, leaving me to pace the house by myself. I fiddle a bit more with the curry, turn the oven off so the pappadams don't burn, light the candles, blow them out, flick through all the channels on the TV, put a CD on, decide it's too cheesy and romantic, pick another CD, adjust the volume, look in on the duck and light the candles again. Just as I'm blowing them out there's a knock at the door. I light them up again and walk-not-run to the door. I take a deep breath and open it.

'Hi.' She's wearing the blue jumper from the other night over a long deep-blue skirt. She's got a bright-pink hairclip pinning her fringe back. She looks great.

'Sorry I'm a bit late.'

'Nah, you're just on time,' I say, stepping aside to let her in. We kiss briefly—our first proper kiss hello—and I follow her through to the kitchen.

I serve up the curry and we start eating. Conversation is slow, but after the compliments and it's-nothings are out of the way I apologise for the other night once again, especially for any assumptions I might have made about the nature of our relationship.

'It's okay,' Emma says. 'Everyone has a bad night every now and then. Let's just see how it goes, yeah? We've only just met, you know. We're still making friends, really.'

I nod. I never thought of it like that. I'm so used to quick sex followed up by disenchantment and crowding that it hadn't occurred to me that there might be another way of doing things. Maybe trying things her way will be less stressful.

There's a contemplative silence for a moment before I manage to change the subject to lighter things, like work anecdotes, favourite books and what to do when you find yourself the owner of a stray duck. After dinner I introduce Emma to the duckling and we let it out to run around the lounge room. We talk all the way through the Sunday night movie and I surprise myself by managing to go the whole night without over-thinking things or being overwhelmed by crush nerves, and when Emma looks at her watch late in the night I'm not devastated when she says she'd better get home.

'You don't want to stay the night?' I ask, ushering the duck back into its box.

'Yeah, I do, but I've got to work in the morning and all my stuff is at my house.'

'Okay,' I say, not pushing it. 'Maybe next time?'

She smiles and stands up. 'Yeah. Next time.' She pauses. 'When?' I stand and kiss her on the lips. She slips her arms around my waist.

'Next week?' I ask.

She kisses me full on the mouth, then stops, thoughtfully licking her lips. 'Okay.'

I watch her go, then quietly close the door and let out a huge sigh of relief. I think that went well, I tell myself. Yeah, I think that went well.

MONDAY

Monday morning sees me back at the mail shed, packing my panniers. Nobody has said anything about my absence last week, which I take to mean that Wayne has kept everyone informed. Dave is conspicuously absent, too. I'd expected him to come over and offer me some faux-conciliatory 'I hope you've learned your lesson' bullshit, but there's been no sign. I count my blessings and finish packing before heading to the kitchen for a pre-run cup of shitful caterer's-pack coffee.

Wayne is staring into the fridge. I reach around him for the milk. He asks me how my weekend went.

'And you *didn't* sleep with her?' he asks, closing the door.

'Nup.'

'And you think that's a good sign.'

'Yeah, I do. It means the relationship's not just about sex.'

'Mate, all relationships are about sex.'

'So you say.'

'So I know.'

'What about you and me?' I ask.

Wayne steps back, arms outstretched, palms up. 'Look, you're a nice guy and all . . .'

'But we've got a relationship, yeah?'

Wayne follows me over to the bike racks. 'Don't you think that sex is perhaps more relevant in terms of your and Emma's relationship?'

I make as though I'm giving Wayne's comment some serious consideration. 'Maybe I'm more interested in establishing a friendship with her. We've already proven that we can fuck. *Anyone* can fuck. It's keeping it going beyond the sex that's tricky.'

'You're a fucking snag,' Wayne says.

'A what?'

'A snag. A Sensitive New-Age Guy. S-N-A-G. Snag. It's like an old eighties word. It means wussbag.'

I laugh. 'How are things with Anthea?'

'Get fucked.'

'That good, hey?'

Wayne frowns. 'So, you wanna come out for dinner with me and Duncan tomorrow night?'

'Remind me which one's Duncan?'

'Big guy. Dreads. Poet. He was there on the night you and Emma hooked up.'

'Oh, yeah. Okay, yeah that'd be good.' I push off into the cool Fitzroy morning.

Back at the shed after managing to discharge my obligations to Australia Post and the wider populace without infringing any clauses or subclauses of my employment contract, I find a plain envelope sitting on top of my rack. It's a note from Sully, who turns out to be the union representative in our shed. He wants me to call him at home to talk about last week.

In the afternoon I wander into the city to check out the stores I visited on Friday so that I can enjoy the cheap thrill of seeing my comic amongst all the other comics and zines—proof that I'm a creator and not just a consumer. It's a low-grade buzz, but I'm easily satisfied. I pick *Godlings #1* off the shelf and leaf through as if I'm going to buy it, then surreptitiously place it on top of other comics and zines to ensure eye-catching prominence.

The last stop of the day is Polyester. I look around and notice the slightly seedy stuff that Emma was talking about: 'alternative erotica' and a shelf filled with bongs and associated paraphernalia. Despite its tendencies toward becoming an 'adult' bookstore, Polyester is still a reliable source of comics and zines. I sidle past the trash-culture video rack to the zine shelves, to engage in some auto-voyeurism.

I scan the shelves for my comic. There isn't much here that I haven't already seen, although I do find a copy of the *I Hate Don Burke* zine that one of the poets was talking about the other night. I flip through it and figure that the cartoon of Don Burke fucking the miniature cow makes it worth the dollar they're asking for. I check out the rest of the shelves and finally I spot *Godlings*, sitting on the shelf above ten copies of *Zines, She Wrote*. It's the new issue. Issue 10. I pick it up. I feel my stomach knot. Gina's put out a new issue and she hasn't rung to tell me about it. This is really weird. I'll try calling her again when I get home. Maybe I'll even go round to her house and see if she'll talk to me. I'm starting to miss her.

I take a look at the editorial.

Last week a friend and I got rotten drunk after work (if anyone from my work is reading this, yes, we paid for the alcohol, of course we did, what do you think I am?) and on the way back to our respective homes, we spotted a guy putting 'This is a Heavy Product' stickers on the wall of the pub. Regular readers of Z,SW will appreciate how exciting this was for me. We tried to approach said gentleman, but we must have spooked him because he fucked off quick smart, but not before leaving in his wake a trail of stickers. The first twenty-six copies of this issue will have one of those stickers as a giveaway, tucked in the back. To those of you who haven't got a sticker in the back of your zine, I have this to say: tough shit. And if the young man who we briefly pursued down the filthy streets of North Fitzroy is reading this, I have this to say to you: I want to interview you. I've watched as you have covered this city with your enigmatic logo, and I want to know more. Are there more than one of you, or is this a solo project? What do you hope to gain from your actions? Did you design the sticker yourself, or is it a found artwork? If you are so inclined, please contact me at the PO Box listed to arrange an interview. It can be as anonymous as you wish it to be—any secrets you want kept, I will keep. But please, satisfy my curiosity and consent to an interview, I beseech you.

In other news, the friend of mine who shared the above encounter has helped me get a job writing for one of this city's ubiquitous free street-mags, so in future issues expect to see various interviews and reviews in their unexpurgated form, laced with the editorial commentary and view-points that you've grown to know and love.

Now turn the page.

She's still referring to me as a friend. Maybe there's hope for us yet. Maybe this is a sign. This couldn't have been finished more than—what—two or three days ago? Even if she'd written the editorial before we had our fight, she'd have had time to change it. But she didn't. Maybe she was planning for me to find this issue and read the editorial and know that she was trying to get in touch with me. Maybe this is her way of apologising to me for calling me a sidekick. Maybe not. But it's a chance, a chance for restitution. I need to respond in a suitable manner.

Back home, I rummage through the junk on my desk to find my half of the Heavy Product stash. I count out three stickers for myself, then put the rest, including the one from the back of the zine I just bought, into an envelope. I put a copy of *Godlings* inside as well, then grab a pen and a scrap of paper.

Hey Gina

Thought you might want some more stickers to use as giveaways. Here's the first issue of Godlings. *I meant to give it to you in person but we kept missing each other.*

Call me some time.

TUESDAY

The waitress comes over and sets three glasses of steaming mint tea in front of us. She squats down at the level of the table. She asks how we are and if we've been here before. 'You have,' she says, pointing to Duncan. 'Did you tell your friends how this works?'

'Nah,' says Duncan.

She looks over at me. I shake my head.

She gives us a detailed run-down of the menu. It all sounds delicious. I listen closely, trying to remember everything she says, but I can't keep more than the meal she just said and the one before in my head, so when she asks us what we want I just repeat the last thing she said.

'Good choice.' She winks at me. I look down at the table, a little embarrassed by her friendliness.

Wayne and Duncan order and she whooshes off to the kitchen.

'That was so cool,' I say.

'Yeah,' says Duncan. 'It's the way it works back in Morocco. No menus at all.'

'I'm definitely coming here again.'

'Wait 'til you taste the food. You won't want to leave.'

The restaurant starts to fill up: a foursome, two threesomes and a lone couple sitting by the wall. I try to eavesdrop on the couple's conversation, but the restaurant is too loud. I watch their body language instead. He's leaning on the table with both elbows, holding a glass of mint tea. She's leaning back slightly, one hand on the table and the other in her lap. They look at ease with each other. I wonder if Emma and I will ever get to that point. I can't wait to ditch the manic double-think nervousness that over-whelms me when I'm around her. I want us to be comfortable, like those two, but for now I'd settle for not making a dick of myself. Things seemed pretty cool at dinner the other night, though. I'm just not used to being the one who chases. I have no idea how to act most of the time.

The door bangs loudly and I look over to see who's come in. I freeze. Shit. It's Goatee Guy. We're sitting to the left of the door, so he hasn't seen us yet, but I duck my head anyway. At least he's not carrying a cricket bat this time.

'Where's Natasha?' he calls out. 'She hasn't returned my copy of *Approximate Life*!' I cringe. Some of the other punters look around to see what the fuss is about.

The waitress walks briskly up to Goatee Guy and grabs his shoulders, turning him around to face the door. 'She's not here, mate. Better go home, yeah?' She smiles as she bundles him onto the footpath and closes the door.

He stands facing the road for a moment before heading towards the supermarket.

'Sorry, folks. Just one of our local colourful characters. Enjoy your meals,' says the waitress, then heads back to the kitchen.

'He was in here last time, too,' says Duncan.

'Weird,' says Wayne. 'Wonder who Natasha is?'

I duck my head and take a mouthful of couscous.

'So, you been getting much work down here?' Wayne asks Duncan through a mouthful of chickpeas.

Duncan shakes his head. 'Not much, no.'

I look up from my half-empty plate. 'What do you do?'

'I'm a butcher.'

'Really? I thought you said you were vegetarian.'

Duncan frowns playfully and shifts back in his seat. 'I'm vegetarian for dietary reasons. I don't think it's healthy to eat as much meat as most Australians do. Plus I have trouble digesting red meat.'

I nod. 'So you're looking for work down here?'

'Yeah, but I don't want to work in one of those fucked-up in-store places in supermarkets or shopping malls. I want to work for a proper neighbourhood butcher.'

'A family business?'

'Yeah, that sort of thing.'

'Not many of them left these days,' Wayne says.

'Tell me about it. The one I used to work for in Brissy went out of business. Fucking supermarkets.'

'So, have you found much?' Wayne asks.

'Well, no, not really, but I did get a freelance gig the other day.'

'A what?' Wayne asks, laughing.

'Yeah, I know, it's kind of weird, but I met these two guys that I knew when I used to live down here. Used to deal for them a little bit,' he whispers.

'What was it?' asks Wayne. 'Someone's pet baa-lamb that they'd nicked?'

'Actually,' Duncan says, setting his fork down, 'it was a dog.'

I spit out a mouthful of couscous. Wayne looks at me intensely and I look back. No words are necessary.

'What . . . *kind* of dog?' Wayne asks, tentatively.

'I don't really know dogs,' says Duncan. 'It was a big one, like a Doberman or something. Tell the truth it was a bit whiffy.' He looks embarrassed. 'I know it's a bit odd, butchering dogs, but it's a cultural thing, really. When I was in Vietnam there were these dog restaurants that pretty much only served up dog, and then there were all the other kinds of meat that they ate as well—snake, rat, bat . . . it's weird how freaked out people get when you tell them about eating dog, but meat is meat, and when there's not so much room to farm a lot of the big animals, you have to get your meat from somewhere. I figured if these guys wanted to butcher their dog, that was their business, not mine. Cut up a sheep, cut up a dog . . . meat is meat. I just really needed the money. I ripped them off a bit, actually, but they should be used to that.'

'They eat rats?' asks Wayne. 'That's gross.'

I'm trembling. My mind is racing. Duncan opens his mouth to answer, but I cut him off. 'Where do these guys live, Duncan?' I'm trying to be nonchalant, but my voice rises to a squeak at the end of the sentence. I clear my throat.

'Oh, just around here somewhere. Best Street.'

I drop my fork.

'Shit,' says Wayne. I look at him. I can't speak.

Duncan has finally picked up on our mood. 'What?' he asks.

'It's a long story,' Wayne says.

I stand up and shrug into my coat. 'I have to go. Have to call Gina.'

'I'll settle up for you,' says Wayne.

'Cheers,' I say, and I run.

I'm pedalling like a maniac, scooting back to my place. I run to the phone and dial Gina's number. The phone rings three times and the machine kicks in.

'Gina, hi. It's Steven. Um, I think I've found out something about Satan. Call me as soon as you get this? Are you screening? If you're screening, pick up . . . Okay, well, call me.'

What do I do now? After that dramatic burst of energy, I'm at a loss. I mean, I don't know for sure that Duncan's dog was Satan, do I? It might be a coincidence. Those guys might have got him to butcher their own dog. Or another dog. Now that I think of it, I don't even know for sure that Duncan's guys were the guys from 58 Best Street. There are lots of guys in North Fitzroy who would know Duncan from his dealing days. I could just be over-reacting. I need to talk to Gina. I'm no good at this kind of sit-down-and-think-clearly-about-what-we-know-so-far thing. I dial Gina's number again, but the machine kicks in. I don't leave a message. This is stupid. I can't just sit here, waiting for Gina to call back. I need to do something.

Usually it takes me ten minutes to cycle to Gina's. If I hurry I can do it in five. What do I do if she's not home? I don't think I should investigate this lead myself. I don't think I know *how* to investigate a lead. I don't even know if this really *is* a lead. What would Robin do if Batman was out of town chasing the Joker and the Penguin started some kind of crazy bird-related crime spree? I think I remember one where Robin dressed up as Batman and scared the bad guys into thinking that Batman was still in town so that they'd all stop robbing banks or whatever it was they were doing. Does that mean I should dress up as Gina and go stand out the front of Mrs Fraser's house? That doesn't sound right. I don't have any of Gina's clothes to dress up in, anyway. At least Robin had the keys to the Batcave, and could get hold of a spare set of bat-tights. This is all pure Gina territory. Without her, I've got no idea what to do.

I'm panting hard by the time I reach Gina's house. I knock once and before I've even lifted my hand for the second knock, Gina answers.

'I got your message,' she says.

She *was* screening. I put that aside for the moment.

'Duncan butchered a dog in Best Street,' I burst out. 'For two dope-heads.'

Gina stares at me intently, her mind ticking over. 'Remember those two hippy guys from the pub? The roadies for the Tweezers? Well, they came into work again. Trudy said they were kind of dodgy dope dealers. She said they'd been in a couple of weeks ago bragging about some huge wad of hash that they'd scored.'

'Do you think they're the same guys Duncan was talking about?'

'Only one way to find out.'

Five minutes later we're pulling up two doors down from where we parked on the night of our first stake-out.

'So what exactly are we going to say?' I ask.

'I haven't thought about that yet. I'll probably make something up.'

'What?'

'I don't know yet. We're here to read the meter, maybe.'

'What meter?'

'I don't know. Shoosh. I'm thinking.'

We head for Number 56, past the wheelie bins scattered across the footpath, and pause in front of the hippies' house. Light from the street-lamps shines onto their front garden, which consists of an assortment of dead daisy bushes choked by knee-high grass. I look over at Mrs Fraser's house. It's odd seeing it at night-time. It's odder seeing it without the gate being bashed at from the rear by a rabid dog.

I follow Gina up the path, trying to make as little noise as possible. 'I thought we'd just sit in the car and watch them,' I say.

'Nah. Too subtle.'

Gina knocks on the door and it swings open. What does 'too subtle' mean? I thought investigators were *supposed* to be subtle. Before I can point this out she steps inside. I pause for a moment before following her in. If all else fails I can always blame Gina for being a bad influence. Aiding and abetting probably comes with a less harsh sentence. I hope.

The lounge room is your classic scuzzy share house, with two grey-brown couches decomposing against the walls below a series of psychedelic landscape posters. They've even got that *Lord of the Rings* poster with Gandalf in the impossibly tall, impossibly pointy hat. The smell of dope and incense and cigarettes is everywhere, and dirty coffee cups occupy every flat surface. Lying on one of the couches is Rainbow-dreads. His head is poised above a red bucket, his dreadlocks reaching down to the floor. For a moment I think he's taking a drag from some kind of bucket bong, but then I hear the unmistakeable sound of puke hitting plastic.

Gina stands next to me, her arms folded defiantly.

The hippy spits and looks up, brushing his dreadlocks over the top of his head. 'Hey,' he says.

Neither of us says anything.

He squints at us. 'You work at the Empress.'

'Are you all right?' Gina asks.

He shakes his head and groans. Then he empties more of his stomach into the bucket. The smell from his puke wafts towards us. This isn't how I'd imagined our confrontation would go.

From the back of the house comes the sound of more puking. I go to investigate, leaving Gina with Rainbow-dreads.

I walk through the kitchen. These guys aren't the cleanest people I've ever encountered. There's a shitload of pots, pans, knives, cutting boards and vegetables in various stages of decomposition and decapitation. A bowl smeared with some kind of brown paste lies next to the stove. A half-empty bottle drips sweet chilli sauce onto the floor. The sink is clogged with plates and cutlery. There's a pot of soggy rice on the stove, next to a wok half-filled with stir-fry.

The puking sound is coming from around the corner. I walk through a small laundry, with mouldy tea-towels and underpants on the floor, and into a bathroom of sorts. And there's Matted-beard—now Vomit-beard—bent double over the toilet, leaning his head on the seat. He looks up as I enter.

'You're the mailman,' he whispers.

'Yeah.'

'Is he okay?' Gina stands in the doorway.

I look down at him. The rim of the toilet bowl is spattered with dark brown vomit. Patches of it stick to his beard and shirt. 'He looks like shit.'

'Fuck, man. My stomach's giving me the heebie-jeebies.'

Gina takes his hand and leads him through the kitchen into the lounge room.

'Barry was just explaining a few things to me,' says Gina, sitting on a beat-up armchair.

Vomit-beard sits himself down in the other armchair, arms wrapped around his stomach. Barry is sitting up now. His face is red, but he manages to talk.

'Well, yeah . . .' says Barry. 'Like I was just saying, about a month ago we scored ourselves some really serious stuff from Manila, you know? Filipino hash. About half a kilo.'

'That doesn't sound like the kind of thing you'd want to have lying around the house,' says Gina in an almost conversational tone. I look across at her, but she gives me a look that is pure shut-up, so I shut up.

Barry frowns, then breaks into a smile. 'Yeah. We didn't want to get done for it, so we decided to bury it. If it's on the old lady's property and not ours, then she'd be the one who'd get busted if it was found, right? So, anyway, we buried it under the old lady's plum tree.'

'Clever,' says Gina, humouring him.

Barry grins again, warming to his audience. 'Well, you do what you gotta do, right? Anyway, so we buried it next door and then about a week later we met a guy who wanted to buy some, so we went over one night to dig it up, but it wasn't there. Someone else had dug it up before us. First we thought it was the old lady, or she'd called the cops or something.'

'You must have been worried,' says Gina, with more than a hint of Jessica Fletcher in her manner.

'We were,' chips in Vomit-beard. 'But then I noticed that the hole was still there, not filled in or anything.'

'And you realised that her dog had dug the hash up and eaten it.'

'Yeah!' says Vomit-beard, sitting up straight. 'And we were really pissed off, right? That dog gets to have all the hash and all we get is the tiny bit we broke off for cookies the night we bought it.'

'Anyway,' interrupts Barry, 'the next morning we heard the mailman arguing with the old lady and we realised that the dog had kicked the bucket because of eating the hash.'

'Powerful stuff,' says Vomit-beard.

I knew it. I *knew* that Satan hadn't died from eating chicken fillets. It'd take something much more toxic than battery-hen flesh to make that fucker—rest his soul—roll over and die. Something like half a kilo of hydroponic hash, for example. Poor Satan. I hope he didn't die with a case of the fear.

'And then Trevor here had an idea,' says Barry.

Vomit-beard grins with pride. 'If the dog eats the hash, then it's got hash in its system, right? So if we eat the dog, then we'll indirectly be eating the hash!'

'Of course the kick wouldn't be as strong, sure, but it'd still be better than nothing, right?' adds Barry.

What? I look over at Gina. She looks as stunned as I feel. Did these guys just say what I heard them say? I think of the stir-fry on the stove. I think of Duncan bragging about butchering a dog. I think I don't really want to hear any more of this. I think I feel sick. 'Uh . . .' I say. I'm not sure that these guys are aware of how ridiculous and offensive they sound. The way they're telling the story, this is one of the greatest plans of all time, the kind of thing you base a movie on or something.

Gina is watching the two of them closely, frowning, but not saying anything.

'So we found out where the body was, nicked it, put it on ice, and then we found someone to cut it up for us so we could eat it.'

'We didn't want to do it ourselves, because we're strictly vegetarian.'

That's it. That's too much. 'Vegetarian? *Vegetarian?* You've just eaten a *dog stir-fry*! How the hell does that make you vegetarian?'

They look at me like I'm a moron. 'It's a spiritual thing, man,' says Barry. 'We were only eating the dog so we could eat the hash.'

'Which is a plant,' adds Trevor, adopting a playschool voice.

'So we're not really eating the meat, we're really only eating a plant. So it's still vegetarian, see? It's a shame we puked it all up, though. Now we'll never know if we could've got off on it.'

I've heard enough. I stand out the front of their house, looking at the fence where Satan used to attack me. It's not that I feel sorry for him, it's just that I don't think anything deserves to be turned into a stir-fry on the off-chance that it will get a couple of hippy morons high.

I stare down the street at the green bins lined up in groups of three or four. Each bin has a house number painted on it. Bin 56, Mrs Fraser's bin, is sitting next to bin 58. I'm surprised these hippy fuckups got their shit together enough to put their bin out on bin night. It's probably the first time in weeks they've remembered. The bin's probably stuffed solid with months of rubbish. There are flies buzzing around it, which is odd for this time of night. Must have something pretty stinky inside to bring flies out at night. Something like rotting food scraps.

Food scraps.

Leftovers.

My blood runs cold. I think I know what's in the bin.

I close my eyes and take a deep breath. I don't want to see what I'm sure is in there, but I can't stop playing the movie over in my head: I step up to the bin and open the lid, and inside, only thinly veiled by the white plastic of a bin-liner, is Satan's decapitated head, staring up at me with its dead eyes, a single fly crawling out of a nostril.

I feel sick. I want to go home. I start walking down the street, away from the bin, towards the lights of the supermarket. I hear running footsteps, and then Gina is beside me, matching her stride with mine.

'Where you going?'

'He's in the bin, Gina.'

'I know. They told me.'

'I saw the stir-fry on the stove.' I shudder. 'I feel sick. He's in the bin. Next to Mrs Fraser's bin. She put her bin out tonight, right next to the bin that those guys stuffed the uneaten parts of her precious Gavin into. Her "wee bebeh".' I feel like crying.

'I know. It's okay.'

We walk in silence until we reach the Tin Pot cafe.

'We should sit down for a bit,' says Gina.

I nod. I could definitely use a coffee. I want to go back to the Imaginary Line and step back the other way. The Real World is turning out weirder than I could have expected.

'What do you want to do?'

I shake my head. 'I don't know. I guess we should call the police.'

'If we do that, we should do it right now. But think about it—if we tell the cops, we're going to have to tell them about the drugs as well. It could get those guys into a lot of trouble.'

I shake my head again. 'I don't care. What they did was sick. They deserve whatever they get.'

'Okay. Wait here. I'll go call Matt.'

I watch her at the public phone across the road. She's out there for a while, long enough for my concentration to wander and for me to start playing the Steven-opens-the-bin-to-reveal-the-rotting-dog-head movie in my mind again. Poor Satan. I never liked him, but it goes without saying that nothing deserves to be treated like that. Maybe it's time to start thinking seriously about becoming vegetarian.

Gina takes her seat again.

'Well?'

'Matt wasn't there. I had to tell them the story about three times before they'd believe me.'

'It is pretty weird,' I say.

'Yeah. I'm not sure they did believe me in the end. They might've just been humouring me to get me off the phone.'

'Well, we've pretty much done all we can do,' I offer.

'We could make a citizen's arrest.'

'A what? I thought that was only on TV.'

'Well, I don't know about you, but it seems to me that the events of the last few days have had more than a passing resemblance to some kind of fictional narrative.'

'You mean like an urban comic detective tale of life, love and getting your shit together?'

'Something like that, yeah.'

Joking about things is making me feel a little better. We order another coffee. Gina stares absently out of the window. I reach over and take her hand. 'I like your new zine,' I say.

'I like your new comic,' she says.

There's an awkward pause.

'Sorry about the other night,' I say.

Gina takes her hand out from under mine and runs it through her hair. 'That's okay.'

'No, I mean it. I'm sorry I didn't help out more.'

'I think you were kind of right when you said I wasn't really doing it for you.'

'Maybe,' I say, tilting my head to one side and squinting.

'I just got shitty because you were doing that thing people do to their friends when they start seeing someone. I hate to think that you'd stop hanging out with me because you've got a new squeeze.'

'"A new squeeze"?'

She pokes her tongue out at me. 'You know what I mean. You're pretty serious about this Emma girl.'

'Yeah, but I don't know how serious she is about me.'

'That's a turnaround.'

I stare into my cup, watching the reflection of the ceiling light in the coffee.

'Just don't do it again,' she says.

'I won't.'

'Anyway, I don't know,' Gina says. 'I guess I thought that if I solved this mystery the way Jessica would have, I'd be happier about it, or something. But I don't feel good about how it turned out. I didn't really fix anything. The dog's still dead and you didn't get your old run back.'

'I didn't really want it back. I think I just enjoyed having something to complain about. To tell the truth, I kind of like the new run. And the union might be able to help me get my leave back.'

'The union?'

'Yeah, Sully reckons Dave broke the rules of my contract or something.'

'You going to go through with it? You're not big on confrontation.'

'Yeah. Might be a good way to start acting a bit more like a grown-up. Might teach me how to stop being such a sidekick.'

Gina looks embarrassed for a minute. 'Sorry about that.'

I shake my head. 'No, you were right. I've just been following other people around without figuring out what I want to do for myself. I think I might try and change that.'

'Well, change is how we know we're alive.'

'That doesn't sound like Jessica Fletcher.'

'It isn't. There's more to me than *Murder, She Wrote*, you know.'

I take a sip of my coffee. Outside the window I see a guy with a skateboard and a canvas backpack roll past.

'Shit,' I say, fishing in my pockets for change.

'What?' Gina looks out the window to see what's going on. I slap a few gold coins on the table and stand up. 'Come on,' I say, rushing out the door. 'It's the Heavy Product Guy!' I start sprinting in the direction that the skaterboy went. Behind me I hear Gina let out a whoop of enthusiasm. I grin and kick into high gear.

In the distance a siren begins to wail.